# NEEDING HAPPILY EVER AFTER

## ELENA AITKEN

Needing Happily Ever After

## Also by Elena Aitken

**Ever After**

Choosing Happily Ever After

Needing Happily Ever After

Wanting Happily Ever After

Fighting Happily Ever After

We Wish You A Happily Ever After

Keeping Happily Ever After

Finding Happily Ever After

Seeking Happily Ever After

Cherishing Happily Ever After

Ever After: Volume One (Books 1-4)

**The Springs Series**

Summer of Change

Falling Into Forever

Second Glances

Winter's Burn

Midnight Springs

She's Making A List

Summit of Desire

Summit of Seduction

Summit of Passion

Fighting For Forever

The Springs Collection: Volume 1

The Springs Collection: Volume 2

The Springs Collection: Volume 3

The Springs Complete Collection - Books 1-10

## Destination Paradise

Shelter by the Sea

Escape to the Sun

Hidden in the Sand

## The McCormicks

Love in the Moment

Only for a Moment

One more Moment

In this Moment

From this Moment

Our Perfect Moment

## Stand Alone Stories

All We Never Knew

Drawing Free

Sugar Crash

Composing Myself

Betty & Veronica

The Escape Collection

## Vegas

Nothing Stays in Vegas

Return to Vegas

**Timber Creek**

When We Left

When We Were Us

When We Began

When We Fell

**Castle Mountain Lodge**

Unexpected Gifts

Hidden Gifts

Unexpected Endings - Short Story

Mistaken Gifts

Secret Gifts

Goodbye Gifts

Tempting Gifts

Holiday Gifts

Promised Gifts

Accidental Gifts

The Castle Mountain Lodge Collection: Books 1-3

The Castle Mountain Lodge Collection: Books 4-6

The Castle Mountain Lodge Collection: Books 7-9

The Castle Mountain Lodge Complete Collection

**Bears of Grizzly Ridge**

His to Protect

His to Seduce

His to Claim

Hers to Take

His to Defend

His to Tame

His to Seek

Hers for the Season

Bears of Grizzly Ridge: Books 1-4

Bears of Grizzly Ridge: Books 5-8

**Halfway Series**

Halfway to Nowhere

Halfway in Between

Halfway to Christmas

## Chapter One

THERE WERE PROBABLY a million ways that Katie Langdon could have told her family about her upcoming nuptials to Damon Banks. Particularly considering as far as anyone knew, she wasn't even dating Damon, and certainly the news was unexpected, to say the least.

She'd actually toyed with the idea of telling her mom privately first, but she couldn't help but feel that there was safety in numbers. Her mom may be slight, but she was tough and even her big brother Logan was smart enough not to piss Mom off.

Not that news of Katie's nuptials should *piss off* her mom, but it was sure to get a reaction. There didn't seem to be a very good way to share the news at all, so Katie made the split-second decision to just blurt it out in the middle of a family dinner. And not just any family dinner. No way. A going-away dinner for her cousin Levi and his new wife, Hope, who had been like a sister to her growing up. The two of them were scheduled to leave early the next morning on an extended honeymoon around the world—or a lot of it, anyway—so everyone was focused on them. No one would really pay much attention to her announcement.

At least, that had been her hope.

She'd been wrong. Very wrong.

Forks clattered to plates. Someone coughed. There was a sound somewhere between a choke and a laugh. She didn't want to look, but Katie was a little bit afraid that her mom had made a sobbing noise.

She sighed, and braced herself as the questions began.

"What are you talking about?"

"Married? Like, married married?"

"To Damon? Are you even dating?"

"Have you *ever* dated Damon?"

"He's your best friend."

The questions, really, were valid and all things that she herself would have asked if the roles were reversed. Still, she kept her answers as vague as possible.

"Marriage."

"Yes, married married."

"Yes, to Damon. We've been close our whole lives."

"Dating is such an old-fashioned idea."

"I love him very much."

It didn't matter that she'd never loved Damon *that* way. It was true, they'd been inseparable since grade one. Marriage would just make them even more inseparable. No one knew her better than Damon Banks.

Even so, her family did not look impressed.

*Yes.* She totally should have waited to tell them.

At least until Damon himself was in town.

Isn't that how people announced their engagements? With their betrothed by their side?

Hell, she didn't even have a ring.

Katie looked down at her lasagna, and took a deep breath before looking up with a smile on her face. She focused first at

Faith Turner, who had a funny grin on her face. Hope's twin sister, Faith had also been like a big sister to Katie growing up, although she'd only recently moved back to Glacier Falls to take over her sister's wedding business at Ever After Ranch, which was the only reason Katie had brought up the whole *marriage thing* in the first place.

"You want to have your wedding at Ever After Ranch?" Faith put a bite of pasta in her mouth.

"No!" It was Logan, her big brother, who objected. "She is *not* getting married. Never mind at the ranch."

Faith rolled her eyes and kept looking at Katie, but Hope spoke next. "Do you want us to change our travel plans? If you're getting married right away, we'll—"

"No!" Levi interrupted. "I love you, Katie, you know that. But we are *not* changing our plans." He looked pointedly at his new wife. "We only have a limited time to do this before the baby and your treatment and...no." He shook his head and Hope nodded.

"No," Katie agreed. Hope had been recently diagnosed with uterine cancer, and her doctor had given her only a small window of time in order to attempt to conceive a child before she would need to have surgery to treat her disease. Their trip was too important. "You aren't changing your plans. But yes, I was hoping that maybe if there was an opening at the ranch..."

"No," Logan said again. "You aren't getting married."

"I am."

She still hadn't looked at her mother, but this time there was no mistaking the sound that escaped her mother's lips. She did not want to see her mom crying.

"It's really not a big deal." Katie knew the moment the words were out of her mouth, they were the wrong choice. She tried to quickly backpedal. "I mean, it *is* a big deal. Obviously. I mean, it's marriage. I know that. But I don't know why everyone is so surprised. It's Damon. And me and Damon are...well, we're me and Damon." She shrugged and took a bite of garlic bread as if to signal the end of the conversation.

Logan opened his mouth to say something else, but Faith stopped him with a hand on his arm. "Just leave it," she said. "Let's just get through dinner, okay?"

Her big brother looked as though he were going to explode, and Katie wouldn't have been surprised. Logan's relationship with Faith was contentious with a distinct undercurrent of sexual tension, but to her surprise, he nodded and turned his attention back to his dinner.

For a few moments, everyone focused on eating and the only sound to be heard was the scraping of cutlery against the plates. Finally, after what felt like an eternity, Hope started talking again about their upcoming trip and some of the activities they had planned. Soon enough, the tension had almost completely lifted and Katie could almost forget that she'd just dropped a bomb on her entire family.

Almost.

Because when she finally dared to look at her mother, Debbie Langdon was staring directly at Katie, a look of concern and question in her eyes. As much as Katie would like to believe that the hard part was over when it came to this whole thing, she wasn't foolish enough to believe her own bullshit. It was only just beginning.

At least she'd have Damon at her side to help field some of these questions. She shook her head and stuffed another bite of food in her mouth.

She really should have waited until he arrived to say anything at all. He'd been her best friend for almost twenty years and apparently nothing much had changed—he was still getting her into hot water.

Only this time, it seemed a little more serious than getting called to the principal's office.

Despite the stress and worry flooding through her, Katie worked hard to keep the smile on her face as she got through the rest of dinner. After all, she was a blushing bride-to-be.

Wasn't she?

———

Damon Banks couldn't remember exactly how long it had been since he'd been to his hometown of Glacier Falls.

Three years? Four?

No. It had been three.

They'd buried his mom four years ago. But he'd come back for a quick trip for Katie's twenty-first birthday the year after. And that had been three years ago already.

It was hard to believe it had been so long. Especially considering not much had changed in the small mountain town. Of course, nothing ever seemed to change in Glacier Falls. That's why he liked it so much.

He drove his newly purchased pickup truck down the highway that led to Main Street. There were one or two new houses and acreages set back in the trees, but so far, it all looked mostly the same.

Damon took the turn that led him off the main road right before heading into town onto Forester's Road. It wound its way up and away from the townsite below to a magnificent hilltop estate that looked over the windy river that wound its way through the valley and held a spectacular view of Jumbo Glacier tucked into the mountains in the distance. It also happened to be the site of his childhood home and the entire reason he was back in Glacier Falls.

Well, *half* the reason he was back.

There was Katie, too.

His *fiancée*.

It still felt strange to think that of his oldest and best friend that way, but he was going to have to get used to it. And quickly.

He pulled his truck off the road beside the main gates and killed the engine, but he didn't get out of the truck right away. Instead, he took a deep breath and ran his hands through his thick hair, almost as if to steel himself for what was outside. Which was ridiculous. There was nothing out there but pine trees, fresh air, and…beyond those gates somewhere, his father.

Damon was being childish and he knew it. He wasn't a teenager anymore, for God's sake. With a shake of his head, he opened the door and stretched his legs as he stepped onto the road. It was heavily treed, and from where he stood, there wasn't much of a view into the valley below. But he knew very well that just beyond the gates, down the lane, was an amazing view. His favorite view, really. It didn't matter where he went in the world, or what exotic locations his travels took him; nothing compared to the view from ElkView Ridge. Maybe it was a sense of home, or the good memories he held of the place, or even just the fact that it was familiar to him. But whenever he looked out over the mountaintops, something changed inside him. Almost as if a switch were flipped that allowed him to breathe again.

And that sense of breath and peace was just beyond the gates.

No doubt the code was the same as it always had been, too. But he didn't press the buttons on the keypad to enter the familiar numbers. Instead, he dropped his head and sighed.

Part of him wanted more than anything to walk into his childhood home the way he did for so many years, knock on his father's office door and say hello as casually as if he hadn't been gone for years and there wasn't a cavernous divide between them. And hadn't always been.

Damon couldn't actually remember a time when there hadn't been a strange distance between them. When his mother had been alive, the gap hadn't seemed quite so insurmountable. But after her death, it was as if the little bit of glue they did have holding them together died right along with her. Those days and weeks after her funeral had been so tense and uncomfortable in the house. If it weren't for his father expressing how disappointing Damon was to both of his parents, and how he'd *broken his mother's heart*, there wouldn't have been any conversation between them at all.

When he closed his eyes, he could still hear his father's voice in his ears.

"She died from a broken heart, Damon." His father's words had come out of nowhere over a dinner of leftover casserole some caring neighbor had brought over. "You left home and she didn't know what to do with herself."

"That's not my fault." Ever since the funeral, he'd tried his best to avoid a conversation like this one with his father, knowing exactly how it would go. "She had a heart attack, Dad. That's very different."

"She dedicated her whole life to loving you, and you just left," he continued, as if Damon hadn't spoken.

"I went to school, Dad. I'm in college."

Anthony Banks shook his head, not willing to hear any *excuses* from his son. "All she ever wanted was to see you settled down with a family, Damon."

"I'm barely twenty years old!" He finally raised his voice, and even as he did, Damon knew it was futile. "It's not my fault that she never got a chance to see that and you know it. I'm only sorry that she was stuck here alone with *you*." His father's face had gone sheet-white, and Damon knew he should stop himself, that saying hurtful things wouldn't bring his mother back. But he couldn't stop the next words as they flew from his mouth. "Did you ever think that maybe she died to get away from you?"

He regretted the hateful words the moment he spoke them,

but it was too late. They'd never been close, but Damon had never purposefully been hurtful. Shame flooded through him as his dad quietly got up from the table and left the room.

That was the last time they'd spoken properly. Not that there was anything proper about that conversation.

Besides a few terse conversations that Damon could count on one hand, he hadn't heard from his dad in years.

Until last week.

He'd memorized the email he'd received barely seven days ago.

*Damon,*

*The time has come to sell ElkView Ridge. It will be formally listed in two weeks' time.*

*I thought you should know.*

*Dad*

There was no way he was going to let his dad sell his home out from under him.

No. Way.

ElkView Ridge was the only place that had ever felt like home to him. The only place where he felt like *him*. And more importantly than that, it was his mother's home. *If it was gone...*

No. He wouldn't even let himself think about it.

Almost as soon as he'd received the email, Damon had called his lawyer to put in an offer on the property. Money wasn't an object. It hadn't been since he'd sold his microchip design in a bidding war with the top computing companies. No, whatever his dad wanted for ElkView Ridge, he'd pay it.

Only the lawyers didn't even get as far as putting in the offer because there was one major stipulation in the listing.

One requirement that any potential buyer had to fulfill before an offer, no matter the size, would be considered.

*Bastard.*

And that was the real reason Damon had come back to town. To fulfill the criteria necessary to buy back his childhood home.

He turned his back on the heavy timber gate, and got back in his truck.

It was time to find Katie. And he was already late.

## Chapter Two

THE TOWN of Glacier Falls was in full bloom at the end of June. It was Katie's favorite time of year to be in town. The townspeople had really upped their game in recent years when it came to the planters along Main Street and in front of individual businesses. There'd been a push for tourism as more and more people in the city that was only three hours away started to look for a place for a quick weekend getaway and some fun in the mountains. Her once small town was starting to become a destination, and although some of the older residents were against the change and the ballooning weekend population, Katie welcomed it. She'd been taking business courses online and was only a semester away from her degree. But more importantly than the piece of paper was the knowledge that she'd gained and the excitement it had generated within her.

It hadn't taken her long to see the potential in a town like Glacier Falls. And she, for one, had no problem with people coming from the city to spend their hard-earned dollars at the businesses in town. Especially considering she had a burning idea for her very own business. All she needed was…well, money. Starting something new would cost a lot. And it was a risk. And, as it turned out, there weren't a lot of investors excited about backing a twenty-four-year-old small-town girl who hadn't even completed her online degree yet.

She couldn't help but gaze at the vacant storefront that used to be a furniture store that had moved to a larger location a few streets back. The space would be perfect for what she had in mind. *The Hub.* An adventure center. With all the tourists coming to town looking for fun and adventure, it was the perfect opportunity to both sell and rent all of the equipment that they could need. Katie visualized mountain bikes, kayaks, and hiking gear for the summer and cross-country skis and snowshoes for the winter months. She'd offer a selection of outdoor wear, shoes, and accessories as well. In the evenings and on weekends, she could offer courses and tours that people could join if they were beginners, or even if they were looking to go out in a group. It would be more than a store, but a gathering place. A home base for adventure.

*One day.*

Reluctantly, she turned away and kept walking toward the falls down the street. With two coffees in a tray, and a paper bag with a special treat that was making her mouth water with the sweet scent coming from it, Katie made the short walk to the park. The town of Glacier Falls was named after just that, a waterfall that was fed directly by a glacier high in the mountains. And as a homage to the namesake, the town had turned the area surrounding it into a pretty little gathering spot, complete with a few benches and picnic tables, and a pile of boulders that had been strategically placed for children to play on instead of the dangerous rocks around the waterfalls. It was one of Katie's favorite places in town.

Her eyes went directly to a shiny black pickup truck parked nearby and she laughed.

*Damon.*

Only her best friend, with more money than he knew what

to do with, would buy an extravagant truck like that. It looked as if it had every single upgrade imaginable and had clearly never been off-road or seen any actual work that it had been designed for.

Well, she'd change that. As soon as Katie got Damon out on the ranch, she'd put him and his truck to work.

"Hey, short stuff. Where've you been?"

Katie whirled around to see the owner of the pretentious truck standing next to a picnic table. Her heart flipped a little, the way it always did when she saw him. It was hard not to react to his striking looks. His thick black hair and deep-green eyes sat atop a tall, strong frame that had dwarfed Katie since he'd finally sprouted past her in the seventh grade. His skin had a sun-kissed glow, as if he'd spent the last few months in the Caribbean, which she knew he had. The scruff on his chin and cheeks was new, and it suited him. He looked both familiar and dangerously different than the last time she'd seen him.

Damon crossed the distance between them in only a few long strides and with zero regard to the hot coffees she held in her hand, wrapped his arms around her in a tight bear hug. Somehow she managed not to spill the drinks as he squeezed her, but the paper bag didn't fare so well.

"You smell good," Damon said into her hair. "Like honey and...honey buns!" He pulled back from her, his handsome face lit up in such a hopeful smile that Katie couldn't help but laugh. She held up the crushed paper bag with Damon's favorite treat from Sweetie Pies and shrugged.

"You really are the best." He winked as he snatched up the bag and took a coffee from her tray.

"I know it." She laughed. It was good to see him. Really good.

"And that's why I love you."

They'd told each other a million times over the years that they loved each other, but it felt different this time. Katie tried not to dwell on it, or how dramatically their relationship had changed since a simple phone call only a few days earlier.

Together, they walked to an empty picnic table and sat on the top of it, looking out over the falls.

Damon didn't waste any time digging into the paper bag she'd brought him. "Hey, this is all squished up."

She shot him a look and he laughed as he shoved a piece of the bun in his mouth. "Still delicious, though."

They sat in silence for a few minutes while Damon ate his bun and Katie sipped at her coffee. Finally, when he was finished, he licked each of his fingers. "Thank you, Katie."

She shrugged. "No biggie. I know you like them and I was walking past, so I—"

"That's not what I meant," he interrupted her, his voice serious. She turned to look at him, and there was no trace of humor in his eyes. "Thank you," he said again. "For agreeing to all of this."

Her stomach flipped as she once again was reminded of exactly just what she'd agreed to when he'd called, desperate and needing a favor. "It's not a big deal, Damon. You'd do the same for me."

"I'd do anything for you." He grabbed her free hand and squeezed. "You know that, right?"

"Of course." She giggled in an effort to relieve some of the seriousness of the moment. "It's all good. Really." She meant it.

"Agreeing to marry me is a *very* big deal, Katie."

*Well, when he said it out loud like that... Damn.*

She shook her head and kept the smile on her face. "Right," she said slowly. "But we're not really getting married, Damon. It's just an engagement." She couldn't help but glance at her bare left hand, a move that Damon acknowledged with a raised eyebrow.

"Don't worry about that," he said in reference to her empty

finger. "I've got all the bases covered there. And no, we're not really getting married. Of course not. That's crazy! As if we'd ever actually be together."

He laughed so loud and so heartily that Katie couldn't help but feel offended. Of course, he was right. They were best friends, always had been. Still, was it really so crazy to imagine that they could actually be together? Maybe it was. Maybe that's how Damon really saw it. After all, he was ridiculously wealthy, insanely gorgeous, and everyone loved him everywhere he went—which was pretty much everywhere. And she, well... she was a small-town girl who'd never left and didn't have any aspirations to leave. She was a simple girl, and always had been. Sure, she wasn't ugly, but she wasn't particularly special either. Petite, with long brown hair and brown eyes, she largely thought that she was pretty forgettable altogether and not at all like the tall, slim blondes and redheads that Damon usually had on his arm, according to his social media.

"It's not that funny," she muttered under her breath as she yanked her hand from his and took another sip of her coffee.

"Katie cakes." He used her old nickname and tilted his head to one side. "You know I didn't mean it any way except that we're best friends. You're like my sister. That's all."

"The sister who's pretending to be engaged to you," she said pointedly. "So you better be nice to me."

---

When the smile slipped off Katie's pretty face, Damon instantly felt bad. He had a knack for putting his foot in his mouth sometimes, and he hardly even recognized when he was doing it. At least, not until it was too late. When they were younger, Katie had been really good at letting him know when he'd crossed a line or gone too far, and they'd had some kind of unspoken understanding about where that line was. But it had been years since they'd spent that kind of time together, and maybe he was a little out of practice.

"I am nice to you." He reached for her hand again and pulled her closer. "And I *will* be nice to you, I promise. In fact, I'll be the best fake fiancé you've ever had."

That made her laugh again.

When Damon's lawyer had informed him of the stipulation when it came to buying ElkView Ridge, that the buyers had to be a family or have a reasonable intention to have one, Damon's initial reaction had been one of anger. But he hadn't reached his level of success by allowing himself to be thwarted by such easily navigated roadblocks. It hadn't taken him long to come up with a plan. A fake engagement was the easiest route to take, and what better fake fiancée than the woman he'd known his whole life and always had his back?

Of course Katie had agreed. Even when he told her that she couldn't tell anyone the truth. Not even her mom. He felt bad about that one, but it had to look real. His father had to believe that they were in love and going to be married. It made perfect sense, too. After all, who knew him better than Katie?

No one.

They could pretend to be in love for a few days, a couple of weeks tops. And when the papers were signed, and ElkView was his, they'd stage some sort of public breakup and go back . to being best friends. No one had to get hurt, or ever know the truth. And most importantly, no one would have to actually get married to satisfy his father's stupid requirements.

"So what do we need to do with this whole…" Katie waved her hand. "Engagement thing? Is there anything special, like going to see your dad or anything? I mean, I suppose he'll probably want to meet his son's fiancée?"

"He has met you. A million times."

"But not as your fiancée." Katie pressed her lips together in an obvious attempt to look serious. "That's different. *Very* different."

"True." Damon nodded as he mulled that over.

"Maybe we should have a dinner or something? We can show everyone how madly in love we are and how it took us so long to realize it, blah blah blah."

"That's not a bad idea."

"I know." She grinned. "I'm very smart."

He laughed. "You are. That's why I chose you." He winked and she smacked him playfully on the arm.

"You *chose* me, did you? I suppose you had a lineup of women ready to be your fake fiancée?"

"There was never anyone but you." He narrowed his eyes and attempted to look as seductive as possible, but both of them dissolved into laughter.

Damn, it was good to see Katie again. He'd missed her more than he realized.

"Speaking of being smart," she said when she managed to swallow back her laughter. "I told my family about us last night." Damon almost choked on the sip of coffee in his mouth. "I didn't tell them the truth," she added quickly. "Don't worry. But you know how Levi and Hope got married and took off for their honeymoon? They left today, actually."

He nodded. Katie had filled him in on what was going on with her cousin and Hope Turner. Just like everyone else in Glacier Falls, Damon had the same response to hearing about their marriage: *it was about time.*

"Well, we were all having dinner last night and talking about Faith taking over the wedding business at Ever After Ranch, and…well, I kind of threw it out there that you might need a date for your impending nuptials to…well, to me." She smiled so brightly, her eyes sparkled.

Katie always had been a bit of a shit disturber. They'd gotten into their fair share of trouble together, and it could be argued that a lot of it was her idea. Okay, *most* of it was her idea. "What did they say to that bomb being dropped?" Damon couldn't even imagine Debbie Langdon's response to hearing that her daughter was going to be married to her childhood best friend when they hadn't actually seen each other in a few years. But the one thing he *could* imagine was that she might not be completely thrilled.

Katie shrugged. "Lots of questions of course, but I spun it perfectly and told them that we'd always been in love and neither time nor distance could make us change our minds."

"Wow." Speechless for a moment, Damon leaned back and took a deep breath. "That's good."

"Right?" She took a sip of her coffee. "Incidentally, our wedding date," she held her fingers up in air quotes, "is July eleventh. It was one of the only dates Faith had available in the coming weeks, and I thought it would give us enough time to do what we need to do and then—"

"Break up?"

She nodded. "Exactly."

"You've got it all figured out, then." Damon shook his head a little and stared out over the waterfall that crashed to the rocks below. It was mesmerizing, even from a distance. "I guess I should set up a dinner with my dad then."

"The sooner the better, right?"

He nodded and was silent for a few minutes. "I went by ElkView today."

"You did? And?"

He could feel Katie looking at him, but he didn't take his eyes off the waterfall. "I didn't go past the gates," he confessed. "I could have punched in the code and at least driven up the drive to see what it looks like. I mean, I don't even know what kind of condition it's in." He chuckled, because he knew it didn't matter. ElkView could have fallen into complete disrepair, and he'd still want it more than anything else in the world.

The fact that his dad wouldn't even consider offering it to him without fulfilling the stupid stipulation of the sale was maddening. And only made him want it even more. Not that he'd admit that out loud. "I chickened out at the gates," he continued. "I didn't want to run into him. Not yet."

"But you'll be okay with dinner? Maybe we should just stick to drinks."

Finally, he turned to her. "That's not a bad idea at all. Drinks seems safer."

"And shorter." She raised her eyebrows and grinned.

"And shorter." He couldn't argue with that. "Okay, I'll set it up and I'll get my lawyer to work up a contract for the purchase. Maybe we can take care of it all at once." It was a long shot that the transaction would go quite that smoothly, but there was no harm in hoping it would.

"Well, you never know." Katie reached out and patted his thigh.

It was a simple touch, and she'd touched him a million times in the past, so it could only be because of the messed-up situation that they were about to get involved in that he felt a flash of heat in his leg where she'd touched him. Still, Damon's eyes fixated on his jeans for a moment before he remembered what he needed to do.

Next to him, Katie was chattering on about organizing an actual dinner with her family, because they definitely were not going to be satisfied with only drinks when it came to this situation. But Damon was only half listening when he put his coffee down next to him and jumped up off the table.

"Where are you—"

"Katie Langdon?" He interrupted her in a loud, booming voice.

Instantly, she was paying attention. Her head swiveled around to see who else was in the park and whether Damon's loud voice had caught their attention. It had. He'd made sure of it. He waited until her gaze flipped back to him and then he dropped to one knee.

"What the hell are you doing," she hissed as he reached into his pocket.

"Katie," he began again, making sure to keep his voice nice and loud. "I've known you for most of my life, and for all of that time you've been at my side. You are the most beautiful, sweetest, and sassiest woman I know, and I love you." Damon took a breath and pulled the ring out of his pocket. He'd picked it up in the city two days earlier. It was a beautiful, huge sapphire surrounded by diamonds. It was big and sparkly, and completely untraditional, and he knew she'd love it. He held up the ring and Katie's hand went to her mouth. He took a deep breath and focused on her eyes. "Katie, will you do me the honor of being my fiancée?"

Of course she nodded, but Damon waited until she said yes, and then wanting her to say it a bit louder for their impromptu audience, he raised his eyebrows and gently gestured with his head.

"Yes!" she yelled. "Of course I will."

Damon grinned as he got to his feet and slid the ring on her finger. It was a perfect fit. Without missing a beat, he pulled her into his arms and hugged her hard, his lips grazing her cheek as he whispered into her ear. "I didn't mean to spring that on you, but I wanted it to look real."

He could feel her smile against his face. "You almost made me cry. That was really sweet."

Damon pulled back so he could look in her eyes. "I meant every word."

## Chapter Three

THINGS WERE MOVING QUICKLY. Just the way Damon liked them. After all, the sooner they took care of the purchase of the property, the sooner things could go back to normal, whatever normal was. As much as he liked to expedite things, even Damon was surprised when the news of his very public proposal to Katie reached his father in a day's time.

Just like his son, Anthony Banks didn't like to waste time, and the invitation for drinks came almost immediately after that.

Damon would have preferred it to be his idea. Or, if he were being honest, Katie's idea, considering she'd actually come up with it first, but he wasn't about to say no to his dad on the principle of the fact that they hadn't initiated the meeting, and he'd agreed to bring Katie by the next afternoon.

He'd rented a room at the Big Rock Inn, because neither he nor Katie had given the details of their engagement much thought until he'd arrived in town. And he didn't want to be too much of an imposition. Besides, word on the street was that Katie's big brother, Logan, was pretty pissed about the whole thing, so it probably wasn't a good idea to spend too much time in close proximity with her family. At least not yet.

The day before, after making things *official* with Katie, they'd spent the rest of the afternoon together catching up. It was always so easy to be with her and even though there was this huge, big thing between them, it didn't feel that way. It only felt…good. No matter where Damon had traveled, and how many great people he'd met along the way, he'd never met anyone quite like Katie. Definitely no one who *got* him the way she did. She'd always had the craziest knack for being able to cut through his bullshit and get to the real him. Even when they were kids and he'd been the new kid in class. Sure, he was only seven, in first grade, but still, he'd stood out from the rest of his classmates because instead of moving into town like everyone else, his dad had insisted on building a massive estate up on the hill, and putting a gate on it to keep everyone out. In a small town like Glacier Falls, it had set them apart—and not in a good way.

At least not for Damon.

The other kids hadn't accepted him right away, calling him Ritchie Rich, and leaving him out of the games at recess. Looking back, it was all minor stuff, but for a little boy, it certainly hadn't felt minor at the time. Sure, he probably could have handled it in a million different ways. But he'd chosen to act out. His target? The cutest little girl in class with the long, dark braids that always waved in his face when she walked past him at the coat hook.

It had started innocently enough, with him tugging on her hair every chance he got. And then, of course, he found more and more opportunities to pull her braids because of the response he got from it. Katie would shriek and glare at him. Sometimes she'd tell him to stop or call him *rotten*. Her response changed, but what didn't change was the reaction he got from the other boys every time he picked on Katie. They'd laugh and elbow one another in the ribs, and when Damon started throwing erasers at the back of Katie's head, too, the boys slowly started to include him in their games at recess. For a little bit, he'd been included. And it felt good. It didn't take long for him to escalate his behavior with her and steal her cookie at recess break.

It had been the wrong thing to do.

Or the right thing, depending on your perspective.

As it turned out, Katie was a tough little girl, and she could put up with a lot. But the one thing she would not tolerate was the theft of her homemade, chocolate chip oatmeal cookie. She'd socked him squarely in the face. Damon had dropped the cookie, but not before crying out in pain. There'd been blood, tears, and ultimately a trip to the principal's office. Damon had the very distinct memory of Katie sitting across from him in Mrs. Gervais's office, slowly eating her homemade chocolate chip oatmeal cookie while he held a scratchy paper towel to his bloody nose and never once taking her eyes off him, the slightest victory smile on her face.

It was in that moment that they had become friends. Because as far as Damon had been concerned, anyone who would fight for a cookie was probably going to be a better friend than one who only wanted to hang out with him if he was mean.

After that, they'd been inseparable and their friendship only grew deeper as the years went on. When they were teenagers, they used to get teased about spending so much time together, and more than once they were mistaken for boyfriend and girlfriend. But they'd never so much as kissed. Not that the thought hadn't crossed Damon's mind more than once. After all, Katie was so pretty, and she made him laugh and…but it had never been worth the risk. Teenage relationships hardly ever lasted, and their friendship was way more important to him than a few months of making out.

Even so, it had killed him when his buddy Jeremy Davis asked her out, and she'd said yes. Katie was *his* and everyone knew it. Still, he had no claim on her, so he hadn't said a word and had instead gone and found his own girlfriend—or six. He never did have the best track record of keeping a girlfriend for very long, a fact that hadn't changed even when he got older, moved away, and went to school. It was a situation that only got worse once he sold his microchip designs, because it suddenly became that much harder to know whether a woman was interested in him because of him, or his money.

*Maybe he was destined to be alone.*

Damon opened his eyes to stare at the hotel room ceiling.

It was a depressing thought. But not a new one.

Not that there was any point in dwelling on it. Especially now, when he was back in Glacier Falls and supposed to be happily engaged. He checked the clock on the nightstand. There were still a few hours until he was supposed to meet up with Katie. With a sigh, he heaved himself off the bed. His laptop sat on the desk, but the last thing he wanted to do was look at his email. It wasn't that he worked so much these days —he had more money than he'd ever need—but he liked to keep himself busy with a few little projects here and there. Maybe one day he'd find something he enjoyed as much as he'd enjoyed working on the microchip when he was in school.

Damon knew he'd gotten lucky with his design—that he still couldn't talk about—and when all the top tech companies took notice and got into a bidding war over *his* design, it had been the best thing that had ever happened to him. At least that's what he'd thought at the time. As it turned out, money didn't fix everything and as much as he enjoyed traveling and having fun, more and more lately, he'd been thinking of trying something new. Maybe settling down and having a family one day…

Damon laughed at himself. First things first.

He needed to get ElkView.

But first, he needed to get out into the fresh air before he drove himself crazy. There was one thing that never failed to clear his head: a good, hard run.

---

"Mom! Seriously, I'm supposed to be studying." Katie groaned and slapped her pen down in front of her. For the last fifteen minutes, her mother had been loudly slamming around the kitchen. Opening more drawers than necessary, slamming them with *way* more force than was required, and openly sighing and staring at her daughter. To say it was distracting would be a gross understatement. "Do I need to go to the library to get some peace? Because I will."

Debbie Langdon placed a freshly baked muffin directly in front of Katie and right on top of her textbook and took a step back to lean against the counter.

"Really? You're bribing me with a baked good?"

Her mom shrugged in an effort to pull off innocence. "Whatever works, Katie. I'm not trying to distract you."

Katie shot her mom a look as she reached for the muffin. Blueberry, her favorite. Her mom was no fool.

"Okay, maybe I *am* trying to distract you, but I don't think it's unreasonable to have questions, Katie. And it's definitely not unreasonable for me to want to discuss those with you."

Katie sighed and tried not to let guilt wash over her. It probably wasn't unreasonable at all for her mom to want to talk about the whole *engagement thing*, which was how she'd started to think about it. But it wasn't really a good time. She needed to do well on her statistics exam the next day. She was in the homestretch at getting her degree. So close, she could almost taste it, but she just needed to get through one last exam.

Taking a degree program via correspondence hadn't been easy, but it would be totally worth it. Soon.

If she could study.

Still, her mother was clearly not going to let this go anytime soon. She leaned back in her chair and peeled the paper off the muffin. "Okay, what do you want to know?"

Katie took a slow bite and focused on the delicious taste filling her mouth as she waited for her mom to grill her. It wasn't until she'd chewed, swallowed, and moved for another bite that she realized her mother hadn't said anything yet. She put the muffin down slowly and wiped her mouth with the back of her hand and turned to see her mom, her head dropped to her chest, silently crying.

*Shit.*

Katie abandoned her muffin, pushed back the old wooden chair with a scrape along the linoleum, and went to stand in front of her mother. Her hands danced around, unsure whether she should hug her or not. Finally she settled for putting her hand on her mother's arm. "Mom? What is it?"

"You're getting married." She still wouldn't look up, so she fortunately missed the wince that Katie was sure she hadn't been able to hide. "And I didn't know."

"Yes you did," Katie said quickly. "You did know, Mom. I told you."

Debbie shook her head and finally looked up, her eyes full of tears. "But I didn't know you were in love. I mean…I guess I always kind of knew. You and Damon were just…"

*What. The. Hell.*

Katie shook her head. "We were what?"

A small smile crossed her mother's pretty face. "You two were always inseparable and there was just something about you when you were together."

"We were best friends," Katie insisted. "We were only ever best friends. Really. I had…" She trailed off, unsure as to why she was defending their relationship when her mother was basically saying exactly what she wanted her to.

Still, it felt weird.

*Very* weird.

Her mom shrugged. "I know you said that, but it always kind of seemed like more."

The idea was boggling to her, but Katie made the decision not to push her mom on the issue. Instead, she played along. "Well, maybe it always was."

That made her mom smile again, but only for a moment before she burst into tears again.

Katie had known that her family wouldn't just blissfully accept her engagement announcement without any pushback, but she hadn't been expecting so much emotion from her mother. Not really. Debbie Langdon had never been much of a crier. Katie could only remember a handful of times when she'd actually even seen her mother cry, and it was almost always when someone died. Not when someone got married.

She wasn't sure how to feel about the fact that her engagement brought out the same type of emotions in her mother that death did. Fake or not.

Katie waited a beat and contemplated going back to the table to finish her muffin, but in the end, she took a deep breath and asked, "So why are you crying? This is supposed to be a good thing." Whether it was or not, she didn't need to go there. Not yet. She already felt terrible about lying to her family; the truth was not going to be easy to tell when it was time. She could only hope that they understood that she would do anything for her best friend, including agreeing to a fake engagement.

"It is a good thing," Debbie said after a moment. She looked up and smiled as she wiped her cheeks. "My baby is getting married. *Married*! And that is a very good thing. There's so much to do and plan and prepare."

And just like that, the tears were dried up and Katie's mother was in full-on planning mode. She moved quickly through the kitchen to fetch her ever-present notepad that hung with a magnet on the fridge and a pen. She pulled out her chair, sat, and immediately started scribbling things down while Katie looked on in awe.

"You'll need a dress, and we'll talk to Faith about the food. Maybe we can get Brody Morris at Birchwood to cater. His food is so good." She looked up for a moment before once more bending her head to her task. "How many people are you thinking? Maybe keep it small, like fifty or sixty people? I'm not sure what Damon's list will look like but that's probably a reasonable number." She thought about it for a moment before nodding to herself. "Yes, very reasonable."

Nothing about what she was saying sounded reasonable at all but Katie did her best to try not to look too panicked. "I hadn't really thought much about it yet, Mom. I mean, it's weeks away, right? And I still need to write this exam."

"Weeks? Weeks! Exactly. It's only weeks away, Katie. Do you know how fast that will pass?" She snapped her fingers. "Like that. We really need to nail down some details."

Katie moved quietly to her stack of books. What she really needed to do was nail down the concepts surrounding standard deviation for her exam. "Maybe you could go through some of this with Faith, Mom? I'm really not too fussed with the details. And I really don't want anyone to go to any trouble. Can we please just keep this small?"

Debbie smiled. "I'm sorry, sweetie. I just got excited."

"It's okay. But really, I do want to keep things simple, if it's all the same to you?"

"Whatever you want, Katie. It's your day. But I will be talking to Faith about a bridal shower."

Katie shook her head. "No way. I put my foot down with a bridal shower." When her mom's face dropped, she added quickly, "Mom, I mean it. Please. Really simple." It would be way easier to break the news that none of it had been real if people didn't make a big deal of it. Katie pushed away another flicker of guilt and picked up the rest of the muffin, cramming it in her mouth.

"You know," Debbie said. "I really do think you and Damon are a great match. He's just always kind of *gotten* you, ya know?"

Katie nodded with her mouth full. It was true. No one understood Katie like Damon did.

"Not like Jeremy," she continued. "I know you've liked spending time with him over the years, but I never was really convinced that the two of you were a match. You know what I mean?"

Katie *did* know what she meant. Very much. But she couldn't have answered if she'd wanted to because she was far too busy choking on the muffin that had suddenly become very dry in her throat.

*Jeremy. Shit.*

She'd forgotten all about him. And sure, it's not as though they were serious or anything. At least, not *serious* serious. After dating through most of high school, they'd decided to keep things casual.

As casual as you could be in a small town.

It wasn't anything serious. They both knew that.

But still.

*Shit.*

---

It felt good to breathe in the fresh mountain air as his feet hit the pavement beneath him. Damon moved quickly, pushing himself faster and farther as he picked up momentum. He couldn't remember the last time he'd gone for a good run in Glacier Falls. Maybe never.

He hadn't really picked up running as a hobby until college and then it was only out of necessity, to get him away from his computer screen for a few hours a day. A situation that had only gotten worse when he'd dropped out to develop his microchip designs.

But those days were behind him, and it had never felt better to stretch his legs and push his body further.

He cruised easily down the side streets before hopping onto the gravel path that wound its way through town and into the forest on the other side of the river for the best view of the falls before working its way back into town and onto Main Street. It was a beginner trail and often full of young families, but it was the best he could do with the time he had. Now that it looked like he'd be staying in Glacier Falls, he'd make a point to find some more challenging routes for some real trail running.

Just as it always did, Damon's mind cleared and the weight that had settled on his shoulders vanished completely as he made his way back down to Main Street. He was just slowing his pace to a walk when he heard his name called out.

"Damon! Damon Banks!"

It was a familiar voice, but not a happy one. Damon came to a stop and turned around, just in time to see Jeremy Davis, his best buddy from school—next to Katie, of course—striding toward him. He grinned and lifted his hand to wave, but Jeremy didn't look happy.

"Hey." Damon extended his hand as Jeremy grew closer. "It's great to see you, man. I've—"

"What the fuck, Damon?"

*So much for pleasantries.*

"Good to see you, too, Jeremy." He didn't even have to force the smile on his face, because it *was* good to see Jeremy. Despite the fact that his old friend looked as though he wanted to punch him in the face. A thought that had the potential to become a reality if he wasn't careful. "It's been how long now? Years, right?"

"You're marrying her? Really?"

*Ahh. Katie. Of course.*

Not that he should be surprised, really. After all, they did date. But that had been years ago. Maybe Damon should be surprised. There was no way Jeremy could be holding a torch after all this time.

"I am," he answered cautiously. "And I don't suppose you're here to offer me congratulations."

"Fuck you, Damon." Jeremy clenched his fists at his side, but Damon had already had enough.

"Seriously, Jeremy." He crossed his arms over his chest. "You're pissed? You dated in *high school*. What the hell is your problem?"

"We've dated since high school, hot shot."

"It's been—*since* high school?" It took a moment for Jeremy's words to make sense. But as soon as they registered, they hit him in the gut. "Like a few years ago?" He tried to keep his voice light. This was *not* going to affect him.

Jeremy tipped his head smugly.

"Last year?"

"More like last month, Damon."

His words sliced through him, which was complete bullshit because Damon didn't have any right to be pissed or hurt or pretty much anything when it came to Katie's love life. No right at all.

*Still.*

"Last month?"

"Last month," he repeated. "Katie and I have a thing."

*A thing. What the actual fuck did* that *mean?*

Damon took a deep breath and forced himself not to react. He would not lose the sense of calm that he'd regained after his run. Jeremy was hurt. No doubt he was a little embarrassed, too. After all, if they had a *thing*—whatever the hell that meant—he would not have been expecting to hear about her engagement. Worse, Damon hadn't even asked whether she was seeing someone. How selfish could he be? *Dammit.* But she'd said yes. Hell, she hadn't even hesitated before agreeing to be his fiancée. Clearly, whatever was going on with Jeremy wasn't that serious or she would have mentioned it.

"Well, I don't know about your *thing*." He emphasized the word. "But—"

"Sex," Jeremy interrupted him. "We have sex, Damon. And now, just like that, you're—"

"Not one more word." It was Damon's turn to clench his fists. Blood rushed to his face, and he wouldn't hesitate to be the one throwing the punches if it came to it. And it *would* come to it if he said one more thing about Katie.

"Or what, Damon?" Jeremy stepped to him and every fiber in Damon's muscles bristled. "Or you'll hit me?"

"So help me, Jeremy. I'll—"

"Jeremy! Damon!" The voice cut the tension and they both turned at the same time to see Katie running down the sidewalk toward them. She wore shorts and a T-shirt. Simple, but gorgeous. The ring on her finger flashed in the sunlight. The ring *he'd* given her. Damon couldn't help but feel a little vindictive in hoping that Jeremy noticed it. "Hey." Katie came to a stop beside them. For a moment, she looked uncertain about where to stand, or more specifically, *who* to stand with. Damon took a possessive step toward her but it was Jeremy she spoke to. "I was looking for you, Jeremy. You weren't at the station, and the guys told me you—"

"Went for a walk." Jeremy looked pointedly at Damon. "There was something I had to deal with."

"Station?" Despite the obvious anger pouring off his old friend, Damon couldn't help but be curious. Had Jeremy become the firefighter he'd always dreamed of becoming? Nobody answered him, but a quick look at the logo on the other man's T-shirt told him what he needed to know. *Glacier Falls Fire Department.* Damon felt a flicker of happiness for his old friend, but that flicker was doused quickly when Jeremy spoke again.

"I suppose you were looking for me to tell me about this?" He jabbed a finger in Damon's direction. "Pretty sudden, don't you think?" He narrowed his eyes. "After all, it wasn't that long ago that you were underneath—"

"Careful, Jeremy." Katie held up a hand. "Careful."

Jeremy looked as if he might try to say something else, but thankfully he closed his mouth and pressed his lips together. He was mad, sure. And he probably had a right to be. After all, it really wasn't all that long ago that she *had* been underneath him. And he under her. Their hookups always were a good time. But that's all it was—a hookup. A good time. Nothing serious, and they *both* knew that. Hell, they'd discussed it like grownups a few years ago. They enjoyed each other's company, definitely. But they were also mature enough to know that it was never going to go anywhere. They weren't in love.

They never had been.

So they had an understanding.

But looking at Jeremy now, Katie couldn't help but think that maybe things had changed on his end. Either that or he was just trying to mark his territory. Either way, she *did* feel bad that he had to find out the way he did.

"I'm sorry I didn't tell you myself," Katie said honestly. "Everything has just happened so fast and—"

"Why?" Jeremy looked between her and Damon. "Why him? After all this time?"

*Because he's my best friend. Because he knows me better than anyone. Because he asked me. Because he needed a favor.*

There were so many things she could say in response to the question. Instead, she shrugged. "It's hard to explain."

Jeremy shook his head and scoffed. "I guess I should have guessed," he said after a moment. "You two were always..." He looked to Damon and then back at Katie. "Close."

Before she could say anything more, Jeremy turned and walked away from them. She wanted to call him back and explain things differently. Or at all. But she couldn't. What would she say? Instead, she dropped her head and shook it slowly from side to side before Damon wrapped an arm around her and pulled her close.

"Well, you certainly didn't tell me about that."

It was obvious he was trying for humor, but something else laced through his voice as well. Katie stiffened in his embrace and pulled away.

"Anything else you need to tell me?" Damon's eyes were serious.

*Yes. There was definitely something going on.*

She swallowed hard and glared at him. "You have no—"

"Not here." He glanced around. They stood in the middle of the busy Main Street. And although no one was watching them yet, or at least not obviously because surely they'd attracted some attention with Jeremy, there was no doubt that if they had a public argument, word would get out.

Katie swallowed hard and nodded her understanding.

Damon slipped his hand in hers and led her the short distance to the Big Rock Inn.

The moment they were behind closed doors in his room, he dropped her hand and spun around to face her. "Jeremy?" It was less of a question and more of an accusation. "You're sleeping with *Jeremy?* I thought the two of you had been over since high school."

She shrugged and walked across the room to the desk where he had a laptop and a pad of paper. "It started up again."

She wasn't looking at him, but she could hear Damon sigh. No doubt the lack of details was driving him crazy. Damon was always detail oriented. It's what made him so damn good at design…and faking engagements.

"Why didn't you tell me about him?"

"There was nothing to tell." That was a lie. Obviously there was *something* to tell.

"So are you guys dating?"

Katie shook her head. "No. Not really."

"Not really?"

Finally, she turned around. "No, Damon. Not really. We tried it a few years ago, but we're better as friends."

"Friends who fuck?"

The force of the word had Katie taking a step back, as if she'd been physically pushed. "Pardon me?" There was *no* way she'd heard him correctly. *Was he really judging her for sleeping with Jeremy?* The thought angered her, and she crossed the room so she was right in front of him.

He shrugged, but there was nothing casual about him. "I guess I just thought you weren't the type to sleep around, is—"

She cut him off with a hard slap across his cheek. "Don't you *ever* speak to me that way again. I don't care who you are or how long I've known you. Nothing gives you the right to try to slut shame me." Damon's hand flew to his cheek, his eyes wide in shock, but she didn't care. Her entire body shook. "I am a grown ass woman, Damon Banks. I can choose who I want to sleep with and when. There is *nothing* shameful about being a consenting adult in charge of her own sexuality. I do *not* sleep around. And even if I did," she continued, working hard to keep her voice from shaking, "it's none of your goddammed business."

Finally, Katie stepped back to give him space, and mostly to keep herself from hitting him again.

"Katie, I…" Damon dropped his hand to his side. "I didn't mean that the way it came out."

She tipped her head and opened her eyes in faux surprise. "And in what way did you mean it, Damon?"

He shook his head. "Okay, I get that it doesn't sound good." He inhaled deeply and rubbed his hands through his hair, leaving it sticking up at wild angles.

For the first time, Katie noticed that he was dressed in running shorts and a tight T-shirt that showed off every one of his muscles. And dammed if he didn't have a lot of them. She forced herself to look away. She was mad at him. *Not* attracted to him.

"I'm sorry, Katie," Damon tried again. "I really am. I didn't mean to be an asshole, because you're right. You're a grown woman. It's none of my business who you sleep with because I know that you are fully capable of making your own decisions and there's nothing wrong with them."

She waited to see whether he might add something else to dig himself deeper, but all he said was, "Katie, I'm so sorry."

She exhaled slowly and nodded but before she could accept his apology, he added, "I don't know what came over me. I just saw you standing there with Jeremy, and then when he said… well…I got jealous, Katie. Really jealous at the thought of you with him and…well…it doesn't matter." He looked her in the eye. "I really am sorry."

*Jealous? Damon was jealous? Of Jeremy? With* her?
*What the actual hell?*

## Chapter Four

"ARE YOU READY FOR THIS?" Damon snuck a look at Katie in the passenger seat of his new truck the next afternoon.

It was at least the tenth time he'd snuck a look at her, mostly to reassure himself that she was in fact sitting next to him and had actually agreed to all of this. Especially after the day before. He'd really stuck his foot in his mouth when it came to the way he'd treated her with Jeremy. In fact, he probably owed Jeremy an apology too. Maybe that one could wait until after this was all finished with. Either way, Jeremy wasn't likely to be okay with it.

But Jeremy wasn't nearly as important as Katie forgiving him. He'd been an asshole and even Damon couldn't believe the things that had come out of his mouth. He *never* spoke like that. Especially not to a woman. And extra especially not to a woman he cared about.

But he had been telling the truth when he said he was jealous. In fact, jealous was an understatement for what had gone through him when he'd learned that Katie had a relationship with Jeremy. His entire body had burned with the need to grab her and kiss her. To *claim* her. Never in his whole life had he felt anything remotely like what had surged through him at that moment. He wasn't proud of it, far from it, but he also couldn't help but question what was really going on in his head and heart that he'd feel that way about her in the first place.

"I've met your dad before, Damon." She laughed and her smile was so perfect that Damon smiled too. "It's going to be fine."

It would be a lot of things, but having drinks with his father after years apart *and* with his new fiancée who he was using to try to trick him into selling him his childhood home was not likely to be *fine* at all.

"You're right." He might as well fake some optimism. "Thanks again for doing this. Really. I mean it."

"I know you do." Her smile was so sweet that it once again made Damon feel badly for the way he'd behaved the day before.

"And Katie?" He flicked his glance between her and the mountain road.

"It's okay, Damon," she said, reading his mind. "You don't need to apologize again. Really."

Damon inhaled deeply as they pulled up to the gate of ElkView. He turned to look at her. "I mean it, I'm sorry. Please believe me when I tell you how sorry I am."

"I know." She chuckled a little. "And I do. Now, please believe *me* when I tell you it's okay. I'm not mad anymore. We're good." He opened his mouth to object again, but she cut him off before he could. "I mean it, Damon. But we won't be good if you keep trying to apologize."

He couldn't help but smile at her faux sternness.

"Okay, okay," he conceded. "But I really do appreciate all of this."

"It's all good."

There was something so genuine about her that there was no other choice but to believe her. Katie was really okay with all of this. He hated asking her to lie for him, but it would be easy. A quick meeting; his dad would agree to the deal and everything could go back to normal. No big deal.

"Okay." Spontaneously, he picked up her hand and kissed the back of it. "Let's do this."

He punched in the code and waited as the heavy timber gates swung slowly inward to give them passage.

They drove slowly up the windy drive, through the pine trees until finally the thick tree coverage opened up to ElkView. Just as it always did, the view over the valley took Damon's breath away. There was a brief time when he was a kid when he hadn't appreciated the view, but it had only lasted a few years. Even as a teenager, he'd never failed to stop and take it all in.

"It's so gorgeous," Katie whispered next to him. "I don't think I'll ever get sick of it."

Damon couldn't agree more with her. He parked the truck along the side of the house next to the garage and moved quickly around the side to open Katie's door, but she'd beaten him to it. She gave him a strange look. "Don't go acting all weird on me now that we're engaged, Banks."

"Who, me? Weird?" He winked and extended his hand, helping her down from the cab. "Have I told you how pretty you look today?" He knew he had because she did. She was dressed in a simple summer dress, white with pink flowers on it. She had on strappy sandals that made her taller, but still so much shorter than he was. And her dark hair fell in soft waves over her bare shoulders.

"You have," she said. "And thank you. You look very pretty, too."

They were both laughing, her hand still in his when Damon heard his father's voice. "Welcome home, son."

*Home. Son.*

It was crazy that two simple words could evoke so much

emotion in him. Katie squeezed his hand in support and it was just what he needed to be reminded as to why they were there. Damon swallowed hard and nodded. "Dad. It's good to see you."

Together, they walked across the yard and stopped short in front of Anthony Banks. There was an awkward moment where Damon wasn't sure whether he should shake his hand or hug him. *When was the last time he hugged his dad?* Still, it felt strange to do either.

Katie saved the moment by smiling brightly and holding her arms out. "Mr. Banks, it's so good to see you. You're looking well." He matched her smile and they shared a quick hug. "When was the last time I saw you?" Katie was still chatting. "It must have been at the bakery." She pretended to think and finally nodded and grinned. "Yes, it was definitely at Sweetie Pies. A few months ago now, wasn't it? You were trying to decide between the rye bread and that new sunflower flax that they've been making."

Anthony chuckled. "I went with the rye, of course. Seeds have no place in bread."

"Oh, but they do, Mr. Banks. You really should give it a try next time. I think you'll be pleasantly surprised."

"Well, maybe I will, Katie." Damon looked between the two of them, his gaze landing in wonder on the smile on his father's face. "If you recommend it so heartily, it must be worth a shot. Come on in, you two. Let's have a drink."

His father led the way into the house and Damon stared in a pleasant state of shock at his dad and his *fiancée*. Maybe this wouldn't be so bad after all.

---

Katie had no idea what Damon had been so worried about. Drinks with his father had gone perfectly. Anthony had been nothing but pleasant and welcoming. With the exception of a little bit of tension between the two of them after the *situation* the day before, everything was fine. And even then, the tension was completely on Damon's side because as far as Katie was concerned, she was over it. She genuinely didn't think that he'd meant anything hurtful about his comments regarding her relationship—or whatever it was—with Jeremy. He'd been jealous. He'd admitted as much. Still, that idea was ridiculous.

*What did he have to be jealous about?*

The thought had popped into her head a few times since she'd left Damon's hotel room the day before. But as soon as it crossed her mind, she'd tried to dismiss it again. After all, this was Damon she was thinking about. He didn't get jealous. Not when it came to her. And there was zero reason to think that anything had changed. Well, except for the whole fake fiancée thing. But that wasn't a reason to be jealous.

"Katie?" Damon elbowed her gently, bringing her back into the conversation. "You okay? My dad asked you a question."

She shook her head a little and smiled as widely as she could. "Sorry. My thoughts drifted for a moment. What was your question, Mr. Banks?"

He smiled amiably and sipped at his gin and tonic. "I was just asking about your schooling, Katie. You're taking a degree in business, I understand? How's that going? It must be challenging to do that correspondence."

"It hasn't been easy," she answered honestly. "But I'm almost done. Just a few more finals and I'll be graduating in a few weeks."

"That's great news. Getting that degree is something you'll never regret." He shot a look toward his son, and Katie hoped that Damon had missed it. But judging by the sudden tension in his body next to hers, he hadn't. "I tried to tell Damon that, but he just wouldn't listen."

"I had a buyer for the microchip, Dad. I didn't need—"

"Nonsense. One always needs a degree. Buyers come and go."

Everyone in the room knew that wasn't the case in Damon's situation. He'd dropped out of college, sure, but he'd also sold his designs for more money than he could ever possibly need. It might not have been the decision that his father had wanted to see, but no one could argue that it hadn't worked out well for him. Still, it didn't seem like the proper time to have that particular conversation.

Katie took one more look at Damon and directed her attention to his father. "Well, I know I'm excited about graduating." She forced as much cheer in her voice as possible. "In fact, I'm really excited about using that knowledge and one day starting my own adventure center here in town."

That got Anthony's attention. He once more turned his focus to her. "Adventure center? What is that exactly?"

Katie spent the next few minutes telling him her plans to have a rental and retail space where she could offer tours and equipment for the blossoming tourism in Glacier Falls to take advantage of.

"I think that's a great idea," Anthony said when she was finished. "Good for you."

"Well, it's still a dream right now. But one day." She didn't bother getting into the details about how she'd need to save for years before she'd have enough capital to even *think* about getting started. "First things first. I still have some exams to write. I will say, the one thing about going to school via correspondence is I've been able to work at my own pace, but sometimes I wonder if it wouldn't have been easier just to move into the city." It wasn't the first time she'd wondered about it. Not that it was ever an option, but Katie had definitely missed out on the whole college experience by staying at home. "But," she continued, "I did the best thing I could at the time and what with my dad just…well…"

"I really was so sorry to hear about your father, Katie." Anthony's smile dipped as he realized exactly what had transpired to keep Katie from moving away from home, at least recently. "I'm sorry I didn't say so before."

"Oh no, Mr. Banks. No need. My family got your flowers. Thank you." Out of the corner of her eye, she saw Damon's surprised look and remembered she hadn't told Damon that his father had recognized her own dad's death earlier in the year. "And I know I've already said so, but your own loss…I'm so sorry."

Anthony dipped his head for a moment and nodded. When he looked up, his eyes shone with unshed tears. "It's been hard these last few years without Leona. You don't realize just how hard, do you?"

"You really don't."

"Well," Anthony said with a lift in his voice. "At least Leona's dream will come true now. She always wanted a big family to fill this house. We weren't able to achieve that ourselves, but it really is a house that deserves a family, don't you think?" He asked the question to Katie, but there was no doubt who it was actually directed at.

Next to her, Damon nodded slowly. "It's a perfect family home," he said carefully. "I didn't realize that Mom wanted more children."

Katie reached her hand across the couch and laced her fingers through Damon's.

"It was a long time ago," Anthony said. "It just wasn't meant to be for us. But maybe for…" He grinned and tilted his head in their direction.

Instantly, Katie felt terrible for lying to the man. But she'd promised Damon.

*She'd promised.*

And she cared way too much about him to risk everything now just because she had a flash of doubt.

"One day." She shrugged noncommittally. The last thing she wanted to do was start talking about fake children to go along with her fake engagement.

"Speaking of ElkView and families, Dad. Maybe we could talk about the details for the sale." Damon kept his voice even, but Katie knew on the inside he was working hard to control himself. "I mean, I'm prepared to meet your asking price, and I know the stipulation was that you sold to a couple."

"A *married* couple," Anthony corrected him. "Preferably already with a family." He looked to Katie and softened his voice. "But for you, I will overlook that little detail for the moment."

"The detail of us being engaged and not yet married?" Damon asked, bringing his father's focus back.

Anthony's face once again hardened, completely in business mode. "No," he said simply. "The detail of not having a family. But the marriage," he continued. "That's not a detail I'm willing to budge on."

"So you mean—"

"Married. The two of you need to be married. Legally. Only then will we discuss the paperwork."

Next to her, Katie could feel Damon begin to vibrate. She knew that when it came to his father, he didn't have much patience on a good day. And this was turning out to be not a very good day. She squeezed his hand and before Damon could say anything to get himself into trouble, she made a split-second decision that she hoped like hell he wouldn't object to. "Well, that works out perfectly then." She didn't look at Damon as she spoke. "Because I told Damon that I just couldn't wait another minute to make it official. After all, we've waited our whole lives, right? I mean, it seems silly to drag it out any longer. Besides, I never did want the big white wedding with all the pomp and circumstance."

"What are you saying, Katie?"

"Yes," Damon added. "What are—"

"We've actually decided to have a really small ceremony on Thursday. Just immediate family."

Next to her, Damon made a choking sound but he recovered quickly.

"Thursday? That is awfully soon." Anthony put a finger to his lips and seemed to mull over what she'd just said.

"It is soon." *That was an understatement.* "But like I said, it already took Damon so long to realize what a great catch I was, I don't want to give him a chance to change his mind again."

"There's hardly a chance of that," Damon muttered.

She turned to look at him, and his eyes reflected complete amazement. She winked and turned back to his father.

"And if it all works out with your schedule, well, all the better, right? Because I really can't think of a better place to raise a family, Mr. Banks. For our own kids one day to be able to grow up out here...well..." She drifted off, and stared out at the valley below that was showcased with a wall of floor-to-ceiling windows.

Almost everything that had come out of her mouth that afternoon had been a lie. But not that.

It really *would* be amazing to raise a family at ElkView. The house was phenomenal. It was large, sure. But not ostentatious. Despite its size, it felt cozy and she'd always felt comfortable there. Lots of timber and natural stone throughout, it had always reminded Katie of a ski lodge, without the ski hill.

Still, despite the beautiful surroundings and knowing why she was lying, it felt awful. Certainly, Damon and his father had never gotten along very well, but he was a nice man and she didn't like lying to him.

"I think it sounds wonderful," Anthony said after a

moment. "Where is the ceremony to take place? Because if you haven't decided on a location yet, I'd love to suggest the patio right here. The view is amazing and—"

"Yes!" Katie jumped on the opportunity because clearly she hadn't thought out any of the details yet. "It would be perfect to do it here."

"This is all so crazy." Damon shook his head. "It's happening so fast. I mean, I don't want you to rush the wedding, Katie. I'm sure that Dad will be able to wait—"

"Damon," she interrupted smoothly. "If your dad wants to see us exchange vows, I don't see what's so wrong with that. And no one is rushing anything."

She smiled as sweetly as she could when Damon turned to look at her, shock written all over his face.

"Katie, I just—"

It was another instantaneous decision, but she did the only thing she could think of to keep him from ruining their whole deception right then and there.

She kissed him.

Katie's lips. On his.

*Katie's* lips.

She was *kissing* him.

Right there in front of his father.

It took Damon a moment—or two—for his brain to catch up to what was actually happening, but when it did, it caught up with a ferocity.

Katie was kissing him.

*Damn.*

All these years just being friends, and not once—okay, maybe once…or twice—had Damon actually ever thought about kissing her. After all, you didn't kiss your friends.

But maybe you did?

*No!*

His brain was going off on a tangent—a wild one and one that could definitely use a little exploring when he was alone—but it would not serve him to forget exactly what was going on at that moment.

But her lips were soft and she tasted like the tangy crispness of gin with a little lime.

He lifted his hand to her cheek and cupped it gently. And just like that, the kiss was over.

It probably had only lasted mere seconds, but it might as well have been hours because despite the fact that the kiss had been chaste and very G-rated, something had shifted. In a very big way. Katie had kissed him. And damned if he didn't want her to do it again.

No.

*He* wanted to kiss *her.* Up against a wall where his tongue could explore every inch of her mouth. Where he could suck on her bottom lip, maybe nip it a little. Where he could feel her breath coming short and fast against his chest. Where he—

"Damon?"

Katie's voice jerked him back into reality and the moment at hand.

He blinked slowly and Katie's face, different somehow now, came into focus.

"Having the ceremony at ElkView will be perfect, won't it?"

*The ceremony. The wedding.*

Her kiss had distracted him completely from what had just happened. Had they really agreed to get married in *three* days? That was very different than a pretend engagement. A real wedding was something completely different.

"We have so much to do." Katie was still talking. Something in her eyes flashed, as if she were trying to convey a message to him. Slowly, his brain caught up with what was happening and why they were there in the first place. "And it will be extra special because ElkView will be our home, too." She flashed a smile and somehow Damon made the connection. He was going to get ElkView. He was going to meet his father's ridiculous conditions and buy his childhood home. And it was all because of this woman.

He shook his head in silent wonder and smiled. "That's great."

"It really is." Katie turned. "Thank you, Mr. Banks. It really does mean a lot."

His father waved her gratitude away. "I know it seems like a silly thing," he said. "And you both must think I'm being ridiculous."

"Well—"

"Not at all." Katie cut him off swiftly. "You only want the best for ElkView. I completely understand." She squeezed his hand. "We both do."

Somehow they managed to make polite conversation for the next ten minutes or so before Katie was able to extricate them from the situation after declining a refill of their drinks. And they'd just about made their escape when his father threw one last obstacle at them.

"Are you both staying at your ranch, Katie?"

"Oh no." Katie laughed. "My mother is a little old-fashioned for that."

"I have a room at the Big Rock Inn," Damon said.

"That's crazy. I have so much house here and you two should be together. I know you think some of my ideas are a little out there, but I'm not completely old-fashioned, you know? You should both stay here."

Next to him, Katie, who had somehow managed to stay calm and relaxed throughout the entire afternoon, stiffened and shook her head. "Oh no, Mr. Banks. We couldn't—"

"I know it might feel strange," his father said, not looking at him at all. "So what about the cottage? It's been recently redone and it's really quite comfortable. There's a full kitchen and really, it has everything you need." The cottage, as they'd always called it, was really the pool house, or the guesthouse that had very rarely been used for actual guests.

It was Damon's turn to object. "It's a really nice offer, Dad, but—"

"But nothing. It's far enough from the house that you'll have your privacy and there's lots of peace and quiet up here for Katie to get her studying done. Besides, with the wedding so quick, it doesn't make sense to stay anywhere else."

As much as he wanted to, he couldn't argue with that. And judging by the look on Katie's face, she couldn't either.

"Well, it has been pretty hard to get work done around my place lately." She shrugged and looked at Damon. "Maybe it's not a bad idea."

"It's a great idea. Here." Anthony handed them each a key and grinned. Damon couldn't remember the last time he'd seen his father smile so much in one afternoon. "Now, I promise I'll give you your space, but if you need anything at all, please let me know."

It wasn't until they were in the truck driving out of the gate that Damon finally spoke. "We don't have to do this, you know."

"This?"

Out of the corner of his eye, he saw Katie turn in her seat and stare at him but he kept his eyes on the road in front of him. Both for the safety of driving, and because he knew if he looked at her, he would want to kiss her again. And as much as that might be a momentarily good idea, it was definitely not a solid long-term plan. Not considering the mess they currently found themselves in.

"By *this*, do you mean the engagement?" Her voice was

tightly controlled, which Damon knew from experience was dangerous. "Or the fact that we just committed to *actually* getting married in only three days? Or maybe you meant that as of five minutes ago, we're living together now too?"

Her voice wavered and now that they were safely beyond the gates of ElkView, Damon pulled over and put the truck in park.

"What exactly don't we have to do, Damon? Because it seems to me that we've just committed to a whole lot."

Katie's bottom lip quivered, but she bit it quickly. He knew her well enough that she was struggling not to cry.

"Hey." Damon turned and reached across the seat between them to grab her hands.

*Was that his imagination, or was there some sort of spark between them when he touched her?* He froze momentarily, but shook the feeling off quickly. He had to focus and, more importantly, he had to remember that the kiss they'd shared earlier wasn't real. *It wasn't real.*

"I meant it, Katie. We don't have to do this," he said. "Any of it. If it's too much, we can just break it all off right now. Actually getting married wasn't ever part of the plan."

She shook her head. "No. It wasn't."

"I know it's a huge ask and—"

"Are you asking me?" She stared at him, her brown eyes wide with innocent question. "Are you really asking me to marry you? Is it that important to you? ElkView, I mean."

*Of course. ElkView. She wasn't talking about them.* Damon shook his head. He didn't even recognize what was happening to him. He never behaved like this with a woman, and Katie wasn't even…well, she was *Katie.*

"Is ElkView that important, Damon?" she asked again before he could respond. "Because if it is, I will do this. I'll go all in. You know I'd do anything for you."

"And that's why I love you." He squeezed her hands. He

had no right to ask her such a thing. No right at all. He was being selfish and he knew it, but he couldn't seem to stop himself from saying, "Thank you, Katie. It *is* important to me. So much."

She nodded and her lips curved up into a tiny, brave smile. "It's nothing."

But it was *everything*, and they both knew it.

"I promise that just as soon as it makes sense, we'll have the whole thing annulled and it will be like it never happened." He couldn't be sure, but Damon was almost positive something flickered across her face when he said that. "And I'll make it worth your while, too."

She laughed and pulled her hands away from his. He felt the loss at once. "Like you'll *pay* me to marry you? Seriously, Damon. Come on."

"No." He waved his hand. "Not like pay you pay you." He shook his head and told her what he'd been thinking ever since she mentioned the idea to his father. "More like, I'll invest in you. Get you the startup capital you need to start the business you've been wanting. I think it sounds like a great idea and—"

"You'd do that?"

It was his turn to laugh. "Are you serious, Katie? After what you're doing for me? This is nothing." He reached for her hand again and held it gently as he looked directly in her eyes. "Katie," he said softly. "I'd do anything for you."

She looked at him as if she were trying to figure him out. A moment later, her face split into the biggest smile he'd ever seen. "This is amazing, Damon. Thank you. I have so many ideas I don't even know where to start. Thank you so much. I'm so happy, I could just kiss you right now."

"Well, why don't you then?"

The smile on her face slipped a little. "What?"

He shrugged, trying to come off casual when he felt

anything but. "Why don't you kiss me then? After all, we *are* getting married."

Katie examined him for a minute and just when he thought she might actually lean across the seat and do just that, she burst out into laughter. "Nice try, buddy. That's a good one."

He laughed along with her before driving the rest of the way down the mountain to get his things and check out of the hotel. But for Damon, that's where the joke ended because even though Katie was trying to blow off their earlier kiss as all part of the act, he couldn't shake the feeling that for him, it had been anything but.

## Chapter Five

FAITH TURNER WAS EXHAUSTED. Her sister Hope had only been gone a few days, on the ultimate honeymoon trip with her new husband, Levi, leaving her to run Ever After Ranch. A wedding planning company that Faith couldn't be less qualified to run. Particularly because where her twin sister was a hopeless romantic, Faith was the exact opposite. She didn't believe in love, or happily ever after, or any of the bullshit pomp and circumstance that went along with the farce that was an actual wedding.

Not that Hope had cared when she asked Faith to move back to Glacier Falls to help her out when she was first diagnosed with cancer. She'd needed her sister, and that's exactly why Faith was there. For her sister. And that was it.

That was also the reason that she put up with Logan Langdon, who'd also been pressed into service to be her *assistant*—or *general handyman*, the title he preferred. And it was the *only* reason, because everything else about the man made her crazy and always had.

"Faith!" She shook her head as, right on cue, he called out her name from across the barn. "Are you in here?"

Of course she was. She practically lived in the *barn* these days. Her sister had restored and refurbished the building into a beautiful rustic facility that had become an increasingly popular destination for brides who wanted a mountain wedding experience. They were booked up for most of the summer with weddings. At least, Faith felt like it was most of the summer. Thankfully, her sister had taken pity on her before she'd left her in charge and hadn't filled the schedule as full as she might have in a normal year.

Faith didn't even have a second to answer Logan's call, even if she'd wanted to, before he stormed through the building, his cowboy boots clomping obnoxiously on the hardwood.

"What's up, Logan?" She looked up from the binder she'd been studying with all the details for that weekend's event.

"You're not really going to do it, are you?" The underlying thread of anger in his voice took her off guard. He liked to spool her up, sure, but he wasn't usually angry.

Faith lifted her shoulders in a shrug. "Do what?" She was pretty sure she knew exactly what had Logan riled up, but it was too much fun to mess with him. She really hated to miss an opportunity.

Just as she'd predicted, his face grew red underneath the scruff of a beard that he'd just started to grow. Despite herself, she couldn't help but think that it looked good on him. Logan shook his head and pulled the cap off his head before running his hands through his dirty-blond hair and pressing it back into place.

"You know exactly what I'm talking about." He crossed his arms over his chest, and Faith actually had to look away. The man pushed all her buttons, and had since they were kids. But damn, he was sexy. And she wasn't blind. "You're not going to let them get married here," he continued. "No way."

"Who?" She was pushing it, and she knew it. But she never could stop herself when it came to messing with Logan.

"Because I'm not sure if you've noticed, but that's kind of what we do here."

"Damnit, Faith! I'm not playing," Logan roared. "There is no way you're letting that bullshit billionaire asshole marry my little sister here."

*There it was.*

Faith released her breath slowly. He really was more fired up than she'd expected. "Damon isn't a bad guy," she said carefully. "And I thought you liked him, Logan. I mean, he's been around Katie forever."

"That was before all this bullshit about getting married."

"So he'd be okay if he wasn't going to marry your sister?" She tilted her head and grinned, but Logan didn't seem to think it was as funny as she did. He growled and turned away. Faith watched as he paced across the floor to the kitchen. "He's a good guy," she continued. "At least from what I remember, and Katie said they've stayed in touch all these years and their friendship grew into something stronger. I think it's kind of...I don't know." She shrugged. "Nice," she finished lamely. After all, as far as love stories went, Katie and Damon's wasn't terrible. "Besides, it's not really your choice. You know that, right?"

Logan whirled around and pointed his finger in her direction. "It doesn't mean you have to help them."

Faith dropped her head and sighed before pushing up from her chair and standing, her own arms crossed. "Yes, it does," she said, knowing exactly what kind of response it would get. "She asked if she could get married here, and...well, Katie's like family. And we have the opening. Of course she can."

Logan stalked back across the room and stopped short in front of her. He opened his mouth to speak, but Faith cut him off.

"And it's not just me who will be helping them." In front of her, Logan's face twisted, and she was fairly certain that if she looked closely enough, she'd see smoke coming from his ears as she continued. "Don't forget that Hope and Levi put this on *both* of us. *We* will be helping them get married at Ever After."

It might have been a step too far.

Logan took a step toward her, his fists clenched at his sides as he absorbed what she'd just said. Faith was ready for him to fire something back at her, some kind of smart-ass comment, or barb that she could easily deflect. But instead, he simply stood in front of her, his breath coming slow and only barely controlled before he shook his head and looked directly into her eyes. "I really thought that, despite everything, you of all people might understand this."

It wasn't his words—although those stung too—but the way he said them that hit her right in the gut. She'd underestimated how he'd reacted to the news of his baby sister getting married. As she watched his handsome face undergo myriad emotions right in front of her, she actually felt a bit bad for a minute. Maybe it had been too far.

"Logan, I—"

"I'm not helping," he interrupted. "I don't care what Levi and Hope wanted." He shook his head, his face lined with a determination that Faith couldn't help find sexy. *Dammit. He really did have the craziest effect on her.* "All the other weddings," Logan continued, "I'm there for. But not this one. No way."

"Logan, you're being childish."

"Am I?"

She chuckled a little. "You really are. This is Katie you're talking about. You can't just not be involved."

He was about to protest again, but with impeccable timing, the subject of their discussion chose that moment to appear. "Hey, guys." Katie waved from the open door of the barn. "Do you have a minute?"

Logan looked from his sister back to Faith and shook his head. "I meant it." He turned away before she could say anything else, not that it would have made a difference.

"Hey, Logan," Katie said as he walked toward her. "Where are you—"

Her words trailed off as Logan pushed past his little sister and out the door, leaving her to look back at Faith, bewildered.

---

Katie looked to Faith for some kind of explanation as to what was going on with her brother, but her friend could only shrug.

"Ignore him," Faith said. "He's in a mood." She waved her hand to dismiss Logan and held her arms out for a hug.

Katie crossed the space and was about to hug Faith, when the other woman reached up and snatched her hand. "Whoa. That's quite a rock."

She instantly blushed and shook her head. It *was* quite a rock. She hadn't really expected Damon to buy her a ring, and she'd *definitely* not expected him to buy such an extravagant one. Or, if she was being honest, one she loved quite so much. She'd wanted to ask him whether it was a loaner, or whether they could return it when all of this was over, but it hadn't really been a good time in the park with all sorts of people— some she knew, most she didn't—congratulating them on their very public official proposal.

"It's nice, isn't it?"

"It's gorgeous," Faith gushed as she turned Katie's hand back and forth, examining the ring. "And you know how I feel about these things. Even so, this ring is absolutely stunning. I love how it's completely untraditional and yet, so..." Faith dropped her hand and laughed. "He did good, that man of yours."

"Yeah..." She snatched her hand back and tucked it in her pocket, out of sight. A wave of self-consciousness washed over her and she suddenly felt untethered and completely out of her depth. "Yeah," she said again. "He gave it to me Saturday. I mean, he would have…and yes…he is…I mean…he did do really well." Her face heated with an unexpected blush as she stumbled over her words. "I mean…he *is* really good. I mean…ahh…whatever."

Faith tilted her head and gave her a strange look. "You okay?"

*Shit.*

She was already screwing this up, and Faith was probably the easiest person to lie to about all of this because it was no secret that she didn't even *like* love. If she couldn't even fake it with Faith, she was in serious trouble.

Katie took a deep breath and regained her composure. Slowly, she released it and nodded. "I am. Thank you. It's just…this is still all so new and I'm trying to wrap my head around it all. It's been a bit of a whirlwind, you know?"

Faith laughed. "I certainly don't. But I could imagine. It did seem to come on pretty fast. I know your mom was—"

"I don't want to talk about it." Katie held up a hand and shook her head. "Not right now, please." She couldn't deal with her mother. Not yet. At least, not without backup. And especially not now that the wedding was going to happen right away. Which was the whole reason she'd gone looking for Faith. After leaving ElkView just over an hour ago, Damon had a few things he needed to take care of, but with time running out on wedding preparations, Katie didn't want to wait to talk to Faith.

"I actually need to talk to you about the wedding plans. Things have changed."

"Changed?"

Katie nodded. *Changed* was an understatement.

Faith laughed again. "I'm sure I can handle it. But not inside. Come on." She grabbed Katie's hand. "It's way too nice of a day to be inside. I need to feel some sunshine on my face."

Relieved to have a little reprieve, at least for the moment, Katie happily followed Faith out into the sunshine.

"Let's sit by the river," Faith said. "I just need a break from this barn and tablecloths and…all of it."

It was Katie's turn to laugh as they walked across the grass to the riverbank. "How are you doing with all of this? Is it getting easier?"

"If by easier, you mean that I now know the difference between mulberry, plum, chartreuse, and mauve, yes."

Katie sucked in a breath. "I hate to tell you this, but chartreuse is actually a shade of light green."

"Dammit!" Faith slapped her hand on the grass as she sat down, but dissolved into giggles. "I *will* figure this out. Also, I better make a note to check the napkins for next weekend's wedding." She shrugged and laughed again. "Honestly, it's not too bad. I think I needed a break from the city and the nine-to-five of an office."

Faith had been working as a paralegal in the city before Hope had asked her to come home to help. Katie couldn't help but admire the way she'd dropped everything, including—according to rumors—a guy, and moved back to Glacier Falls without hesitation.

"Although," Faith continued, "it would be nice to get outside and actually enjoy the mountains a little bit. What's the point in having this amazing backyard if I don't have time to enjoy it? And I think I'm actually getting paler." She shook her head. "It's practically summer—I should have a tan, or at least the start of one, not the other way around. I spend so much time inside or out at night that people are going to think I'm a vampire."

There was no way anyone would mistake Faith for anything else besides beautiful. She and Hope had always had tall, perfectly curvy figures that along with their long blonde hair and blue eyes made them some of the prettiest girls in town. When they were growing up, Katie had spent far too many hours longing for hair just as blonde as theirs. The day her mother had caught her trying to bleach out her own dark locks with peroxide was definitely not one of her proudest moments. But she'd only been ten and didn't know that the only thing peroxide would do to her hair was turn it orange. Thankfully her mother had taken pity on her and hadn't let her go around with orange streaks, but instead had gone to the store to buy a box of dye. She'd spent hours covering her color mistake and drying Katie's tears.

Thinking about her mom again gave Katie another twinge of guilt. She shook her head and changed the subject. "We should go mountain biking."

Faith turned and stared at her. "Mountain biking? It's been years since I was on a bike."

"Well then, you're in luck." Katie grinned. "Because it's just like riding a bike. And I'm sure we could round up a few to go hit a trail one afternoon. It would be fun. I mean, if you can spare a half a day somewhere?"

"I should be able to make that happen." She nodded and then smiled. "Yes. Let's make that happen. Now, tell me what this change to your wedding plans is."

"Right." Katie forced a smile on her face. "About that… well, we need to change the date a little bit."

Faith's face twisted up into mild panic. "Okay. I mean, I could see what I could do. When are you thinking?"

"Thursday."

Her friend's mouth opened and shut before she finally swallowed firmly. "Thursday? Like, this Thursday?"

Katie nodded. "Something super small, up at ElkView. Just a ceremony and a champagne toast. That's it. Okay? Easy?"

"Does your mom know yet?"

Katie shook her head. "I'm telling them tonight. At dinner. You're coming, right?"

Katie wouldn't have been surprised if Faith bailed out of dinner. Hell, she would have if she could help it. Telling her family about the wedding was bad enough. But to tell them it was later *this* week…

Finally, Faith nodded and smiled. "Okay, I'll come to dinner."

"And the wedding?"

"Thursday, you say?" Katie nodded and Faith blew out a breath. "Okay. No problem. After all, I *am* a professional." Faith attempted a straight face, but when a moment later she asked, "How do you feel about the color chartreuse?" she cracked and they both dissolved into giggles.

## Chapter Six

MOST OF THE TIME, Faith was grateful for the dinner invitations at the Langdon ranch. With Hope and Levi gone on their trip, she had no real family around and the Langdons—with the exception of Logan, who only drove her crazy—were as close to family as she could get. So when the invitation came to join them for a dinner, she jumped at it. And it was always a good time.

Mostly.

When she'd accepted Debbie's invite a few days before, she hadn't realized that it would also be the first time that Katie brought Damon over to the house since announcing their engagement, nor did she know that the rest of the family hadn't been told that the actual wedding was in three days' time. No, she only realized that once it was too late. At least, she was pretty sure it was too late to make an excuse to leave once she was sitting at the dining room table.

The betrothed were late to get there, something about having to check Damon out of the Big Rock Inn. Not that it mattered what the excuse was; Logan was agitated from the moment the other man walked into the room, and Faith was pretty sure that his attitude was only going to get worse. Damon wouldn't be able to say anything right.

"Calm down," she whispered to Logan, who'd somehow ended up sitting next to her. He was practically vibrating. His knee bounced up and down so intensely that Faith thought he might actually knock the table and send Debbie's dishes flying if he didn't settle down. "You're going to make a scene."

"It's not me who should be worried about making a scene." He spoke out of the side of his mouth, not taking his eyes off Damon, who was doing his best to avoid looking in Logan's direction. No doubt he could feel the completely unwarranted rage radiating off his fiancée's brother. "He needs to be worried."

"Logan," Faith hissed. "Seriously." Before she could stop herself, she put her hand on Logan's thigh and pressed it down, squeezing gently.

He froze and turned to look first at Faith, and then down at her hand on his leg. He looked up at her again, a look of question in his eyes. But before either of them could make more out of the simple touch than what it was, she snatched her hand back and tucked it into her lap.

"I'm so glad you all could finally make it." Debbie chose that moment to walk into the dining room, a platter of roast chicken in her hands. The smell of it made Faith's mouth water and for at least a moment, everyone was distracted from the giant elephant in the room. That is, until Debbie set the chicken down, looked directly at Damon, and addressed it head on. "So, I finally get to congratulate you in person."

Once again, Logan started to vibrate and Faith shook her head slightly. She looked to Katie to offer her a small smile of support.

"Thank you, Mrs. Langdon. I—"

"Call me Debbie." She interrupted him. "After all, we're finally going to be family." Debbie sat, a genuine smile on her face. "I mean, I feel like you've been family for years. But this..." She gestured between her daughter and her new fiancé. "This is special. I'm very excited."

Faith could see Katie visibly relax. Now if only her brother could do the same.

"I know it all happened so quickly," Damon began.

*That was an understatement.* Faith looked pointedly at the basket of rolls she'd been handed.

"But it's just one of those things and once we made it official, we just didn't want to wait," Damon continued.

"Speaking of not wanting to wait."

Faith froze, acutely aware of Logan sitting next to her. He was *not* going to be happy.

"We've decided to push the wedding date up."

"Up?" Debbie asked the question while, next to Faith, Logan choked a little on a roll. "What do you mean, up?"

"We've decided to have an intimate ceremony at ElkView." She paused. "On Thursday."

Just as Faith had predicted, Logan reacted instantly. "What the actual—"

"It's what we want." Katie cut him off smoothly.

"It's insane."

"It's not. And Faith has agreed to help out with all the details."

Faith felt more than saw how Logan felt about his little sister's upcoming nuptials.

"You did?"

Faith turned to him finally. "Of course I did. And I would think that you'd be pleased about it."

"Pleased?"

"Yes." She smiled as innocently as she could. "Since the wedding isn't at Ever After, you're not *required* to help."

"Logan, I really hope you can be okay with this." Katie's

voice was soft, and Faith watched as Logan's face softened at his little sister's plea. "I need you there. Please."

He nodded after a moment. "Of course."

"I think it's exciting," Debbie jumped in with a small clap of her hands. "I mean, it's crazy fast. But with Faith to help out, I know it'll be great."

"I really want to thank you, Faith." Damon spoke up. "You're working so hard to make this happen quickly and I know you're still new to the whole thing."

"Don't worry about it." She waved her hand. "It's my pleasure. Besides, it gives me a chance to practice all my new mad wedding skills."

Everyone laughed, including Logan, who actually snorted next to her. She turned to glare at him. "What? I am figuring it all out."

"Right," Logan said, trying not to choke. "You have *mad* wedding skills."

"I do."

She didn't, but the last thing she needed was Logan pointing it out to her.

She turned her attention back to Damon and Katie. "I promise I will plan the perfect wedding for you two. Right down to the dress. And speaking of the dress…"

"Oh no." Katie waved her hand.

"Oh yes," Faith insisted. "You need a dress. Hope would kill me if she knew I let you get married in some random sundress. We're going to the city tomorrow," she continued. "And we're going to buy you the perfect dress." Faith knew she was talking out of her ass, especially considering that she had no idea where to even begin looking for the right wedding dress. But she'd figure it out by the morning. "Debbie, you should come, too."

Just as Faith was hoping she would, Debbie jumped at the chance. "Yes!"

"But I have an exam in the morning."

"Perfect. You'll already be in the city." Faith winked, and Katie laughed with a resigned shake of her head.

"It'll be great," Damon said. "You deserve the most beautiful dress. Go, have fun."

Katie's face showed myriad emotions, and there was some kind of look exchanged between the two of them that Faith couldn't quite figure out. But then again, she was definitely no expert on relationships, and finally Katie smiled. "Okay," she said. "It sounds like fun."

"Great! As for the rest of the details…"

"Honestly, Faith. You go ahead and do whatever you think. We completely trust you."

Damon nodded. "We do."

Damon reached over and took Katie's hand in hers. It was such a sweet gesture, and Faith couldn't help but feel the slightest flicker of…what? *Was it jealousy? Want?*

*No.* That was ridiculous. She didn't want what they had. She didn't want a relationship. She definitely didn't want to get married and sure, they thought they were in love. But despite the occupation she found herself in, Faith still didn't believe that love was a real thing. At least not a real thing that would last.

She forced a smile on her face. "Well then, I'll do everything I can to make sure it's a beautiful day and you won't need to worry about a thing." Secretly, Faith hoped that she *could* pull it off. Most of the weddings that season had been lined up by Hope before she'd gotten sick and taken off on her whirlwind honeymoon. They'd been designed and planned and basically completely thought-out already. All Faith had to do was execute them. She was great at following instructions when it came to all this. But actually *planning* a wedding? That might be a stretch. And as much as she didn't want to admit it, and no matter what she'd just told him, she was really going to need Logan to help out for this one.

Faith glanced over at him and, just as she'd expected, his mouth was pressed into a hard line. His jaw clenched and she could see the little muscles flexing as he was clearly working hard not to say what he really wanted to. Despite herself, Faith couldn't help but notice just how damn good-looking the man was when he was being fiercely protective of his little sister. Sure, it was annoying, and Logan definitely *was* annoying. *But...*

She looked away and focused on her dinner before she could let her brain entertain any thoughts about Logan that didn't involve how much of a pain in the ass he was.

Katie dumped an arm full of dirty dishes onto the kitchen counter and let out the breath she felt like she'd been holding since dinner had started. She had definitely not been looking forward to telling her family about the pushed-up wedding date. She put both hands on the edge of the sink and dropped her head down.

"So that wasn't so bad, was it?" Damon stacked another load of dishes next to hers as he followed her into the kitchen. "Your mom actually handled things better than I thought. She seems excited."

"She is." Katie turned to look at him. "Did you know she actually told me that she'd always expected us to end up together? Isn't that crazy?"

"Is it?" He shrugged so casually that for the slightest second Katie actually thought that Damon felt the same way. But then he quickly laughed. "Ha! Can you imagine?" He shook his head. "That's crazy talk."

"Right?" It was beyond strange, but Katie felt a flash of

disappointment go through her. *It wasn't really crazy to imagine them together, was it?*

"And it sounds like Faith is going to handle all the details." Damon had already moved on in the conversation. "And... well, Logan is..."

"Logan is Logan. He wasn't going to be happy no matter what." She turned around to face him and was startled by how close he stood. A shiver went through her body at his nearness, but he didn't seem to notice. And if he did, it didn't bother him to be close to her.

Not that it *bothered* her. Quite the opposite.

She shook her head quickly in an effort to clear her thoughts. *This is fake*, Katie reminded herself. *It's all fake.*

Even if the kiss they'd shared earlier had felt very, very real.

She'd tried to laugh it off because what else could she do? It's not as if she could tell him that when his lips touched hers something had happened inside her. Something that had *never* happened before. It was like a full-body shiver, but instead of being cold, it was the exact opposite. His lips had lit her up in a way that had sparked a very dangerous fire within her. And even though it had only lasted a moment, she was certain that if she closed her eyes right now, she would still be able to taste him.

But nothing about that would be a good idea, so Katie forced herself to keep her eyes open and directly on Damon, who looked at her strangely.

"Are you okay?"

She nodded and smiled. "Fine. It's just that all this is so..." She sighed. "It's a lot and I still have to pack."

*Pack.* Yes. She had to pack. It was the perfect way to get a little space and clear her head.

"You know what?" She wiggled to the side and moved toward the hall. "If you start the dishes, I can go throw a few things in a bag so we can get out of here a little faster. I think it'll be easier to…well, you know…*lie*," she whispered the last word, "if we limit the time we spend around my family."

He nodded, but if she didn't know better, Katie might have thought that he looked a little disappointed. "No problem. I'll take care of the cleanup. You pack."

"Pack for what?" They both spun around to see Logan in the door with the remaining dishes stacked in his arms. "Where are you going?"

It was clear that Logan still wasn't happy about their engagement. The last thing she needed to deal with was a scene with her big brother. "Damon's dad has generously offered us the guesthouse to stay in." Katie grinned and tried to keep her voice light. "There's just so much more room up at ElkView. We thought it might get crowded here and well, with the wedding in a few days, it doesn't really make sense for Damon to stay at the hotel, so…"

Damon and Katie waited and watched Logan carefully. Katie was half convinced that her brother might actually take a swing at Damon, but to her surprise, he shrugged.

"Makes sense."

"It does?"

Logan forced out a chuckle. "Of course it does." He waved at her. "Go. Pack. I'll help Damon with the dishes."

A sliver of panic threaded through her, but Katie had no idea how to get out of leaving them alone together. Not without it looking suspicious. She looked to Damon, who nodded and smiled.

"Okay," she said on an exhale. "Sounds good." Right before she turned to leave, she had a thought and took two quick steps across the room to press her lips to Damon's cheek. "I'll see you soon."

His eyes held hers for a beat as she pulled away. Something in the way he looked at her caused a fluttering sensation low in her belly.

*Stop that!*

She really needed to get that under control. The last thing she needed to complicate everything even more was to actually have any kind of romantic feelings for her husband-to-be.

The moment she was alone, she dropped her head and took three quick breaths, forcing herself to calm down. It was just Damon. The same Damon he'd always been. Their relationship was exactly the same as it had always been. *Friends.* There was nothing between them. It was pretend. *That was all.*

And that's what she kept telling herself as she threw her clothes and her school books into a duffel bag. By the time she was done packing and had rejoined the others in the living room, just in time to say goodnight, she'd actually convinced herself of it. They were only friends. There was nothing between them. Nothing real. Just a little lie that they needed to keep playing at for a little bit longer and then they could go right back to being Damon and Katie, best friends.

They said their good-byes and were almost home free as they walked away from the house toward Damon's truck and freedom from what had been the hardest part of the whole deception so far when Damon paused with his hand on the truck door he'd been about to open for her. "They're all watching," he said through his smile. "Let's give them something to watch."

Before Katie could ask him what he meant, he pulled her close with one hand while the other cupped her cheek. And then he was kissing her. *Really* kissing her. In an instant, everything fell away and Katie forgot about the fact that her family was watching them, or that it wasn't supposed to be real. Her knees actually buckled a little, but Damon held her tight. He tasted faintly of the coffee they'd had after their meal as his tongue slipped between her lips and found hers. There was nothing *pretend* about this kiss. Absolutely. Nothing.

It was as real as it got and when he finally pulled his mouth away from hers, she was completely speechless. Her breath came in short bursts and her heart raced.

"That was perfect," Damon whispered against her lips before pulling back, and opening the truck door for her. He helped her up and inside, and somehow she managed to regain her senses long enough to buckle her seat belt and wave out the window as they drove away.

It *was* perfect, all right. Katie swallowed hard and forced herself not to look at him.

And that was going to be a problem.

---

*Okay, maybe he didn't have to kiss her.*

But with her family standing there watching them, it wasn't a bad idea to make sure that they really looked like a young couple in love, right?

That was the story Damon told himself all the way back up the mountain to ElkView while they drove in silence. He'd kissed her just to keep up the act. Nothing more. It had absolutely nothing to do with the fact that ever since the first time his lips touched hers, his entire body had yearned to have her in his arms again.

*No.* It had *nothing* to do with that.

And he was a big fat liar.

Damon bit his lip and said a series of completely inappropriate things to himself in his head as he punched in the code for the gate and steered the truck the short distance to the cottage. He was being an asshole. A selfish asshole, which, as far as he was concerned, was the worst kind. It was bad enough he'd asked Katie to participate in this ridiculous lie for his personal benefit, but to confuse the situation even further by being so completely attracted to her? That was over the line. He needed to rein himself in. And fast. It wasn't fair to Katie.

"Here we are," he said in an overly cheerful voice that sounded brash and obnoxious in the silence of the truck. "Can I grab your things?"

She looked at him for the first time since they'd left the ranch and shook her head slightly, as if she'd just come out of a daze. "It's okay. I've got it."

Damon jumped out of the truck and ran around to the back to grab her bags, at the same moment that she got there.

"I've got them, Damon. Really."

"No." He reached for her duffel at the same time she did. "I in—"

His hand touched hers and a shock went through him at what should have been an innocent touch. Her fingers lingered on his hand. He looked first at her hand, and then into her brown eyes, wide with shock. *Did she feel it too? Was it…what…*

"Okay," she said quickly as she pulled her hand back and broke whatever little spell had come over them. "If you insist. You're welcome to do all the heavy lifting." Her voice was light and teasing and totally normal.

*Maybe he'd imagined it. Maybe there was nothing there.*

It had been years since he'd actually been in the cottage, but it was almost exactly as Damon remembered it. The entire guesthouse consisted of one large room with a small but well-equipped kitchen tucked into one corner, with a table and two chairs that would be perfect for Katie to set up a studying station. The rest of the room was filled with a large couch and two oversized chairs facing the glass doors that looked out to a large covered deck and the view that was worth a million bucks. Behind the kitchen was the one bedroom and bathroom that completed the space that was really the size of a small apartment.

It would have been perfect for one, or even a couple. A *real* couple. But as Damon pushed open the door to let Katie enter first, the problem with the space became clear immediately.

One bedroom. And they were definitely *not* a real couple.

"I'll sleep on the—"

"You take the bed—"

They spoke at the same time.

Katie laughed. "I'm not taking the bed while you're out here. It's your house. That's silly."

"You're doing this for me, Katie. There's no way I'm going to make you sleep on the couch."

He watched as Katie walked through the kitchen. She ran her hand along the backs of the wooden chairs as she moved slowly and Damon was hit with a blast of deja vu. She'd done exactly the same thing, the last time they'd been in the guest-house together. They'd been teenagers and they'd been looking for alcohol they could sneak out to a bush party that was happening that Friday. Damon was sure his parents wouldn't notice any extra they had in the cottage if it went missing, so together, they'd snuck in. Even back then, Katie had walked through the small space with a dreamy look in her eyes.

"Could you imagine if this was your house?" She'd spun with her arms outstretched. "Like, *all* yours? You didn't have to share with anyone."

"It's pretty small." Damon had laughed.

"Are you kidding?" She turned on her heel to stare at him. "It's perfect. I can imagine it now." She squeezed her eyes shut and a small smile crept up her face. "The perfect apartment, with no annoying big brother barging in when I'm listening to music, and no parents telling me what to do or when to go to bed." She opened her eyes again. "Maybe one day, right?"

Damon shook his head clear of the memory. "One day" was upon them.

He closed the door behind him as Katie walked through into the bedroom and flicked on the light. "It's a king-sized bed," she called out. "We could share."

His body reacted immediately and dramatically at her

suggestion. *There was no way.* "Share?" He hoped his voice didn't betray every racing thought going through his mind because the moment she'd offered up the suggestion, his brain had gone directly to imagining her in the middle of that king-sized bed, her arms behind her head, her long, dark hair spread out on the pillow beneath her, and her perfect little body completely naked and—

"Sure," she said, interrupting his thought before he could get carried away with it. "Why not? We've shared beds before."

They had. That was before.

Before he'd kissed her. Before she was *Katie.*

Katie appeared in the doorway with a smile on her face. "I'm sure we can handle it," she said. "After all, we're getting married in a few days." She waved her ring in the air.

Damon forced a lightness into his voice. "Of course we can. We can handle anything."

## Chapter Seven

*WE CAN HANDLE ANYTHING.*

Damon's words, like a bad joke, repeated themselves over and over in Katie's head the next morning, dominating her thoughts as she drove into the city when what should have been in her thoughts were the terms and definitions for her last exam.

*We can handle anything.*

They could. *She* could.

Of course Katie could handle anything. *Like focusing on her exam.*

She was strong. She'd always been strong and independent, and when she made her mind up about something, she did it. No wavering.

She could handle *anything*.

Except sleeping in a bed with Damon Banks.

And it was driving her crazy. Or maybe that was the lack of sleep or the stress of the pending exam—never mind the wedding—talking. But whatever it was, even after only one night sleeping next to Damon, only inches from his hard, toned body, Katie knew for a fact that it was going to make her crazy. For whatever reason, maybe it was the kiss…or the other kiss… or…whatever, she had somehow become completely and totally illogically attracted to her best friend. Not that her body cared at all about logic. Not when it came to Damon.

Because whenever Damon laid down next to her under the feather duvet in that king bed, that might as well have been a single for how small it felt with both of them in it, her entire body lit up like a firecracker ready to explode. The only way she could deal with her full-body betrayal was by squeezing her eyes shut and taking deep breaths as she ran through economic theories and calculus functions in her mind while pretending to sleep. She certainly hadn't gotten much sleep that way, but the extra studying—if you could call it that—would hopefully pay off at her exam.

By the time she left the exam center a few hours later, she felt confident that even with her complete lack of sleep, she'd totally nailed it. The sense of relief she felt as she walked to her car was immense. She'd done it. She was going to get her degree!

And now, with her degree, and Damon's investment…she was finally going to have her store! Katie didn't want to dwell on the reason she'd have the funds to start up her shop because if she thought about it too long, it made her feel a little seedy. Not that what she was doing with Damon was wrong. Not really.

Okay, the lie was probably wrong. And maybe taking money in exchange for helping him lie was technically wrong. But it's not as if Damon were just anyone. He was *Damon*. He was her best friend. She'd help him out even if there were no money involved, just like she knew he'd help her.

The fact that she couldn't seem to get him off her mind for completely unrelated reasons was…well…just a *thing*.

Not that there was any time to either celebrate her achievement or think about the *thing.* She glanced at the time on her phone.

She was supposed to be meeting Faith and her mother at a bridal store in less than thirty minutes.

*Out of the pan and into the fire.*

She shook her head with a laugh. *Might as well get it done with.*

The final exam seemed like a small hurdle compared to what was in front of her: buying a wedding dress.

A few minutes later, Katie found the store and paused before pulling open the heavy glass door and stepping inside. It seemed completely surreal. She was just about to chicken out completely when Faith's voice rang out.

"Hey. There you are."

Katie spun around, saved from her thoughts as Faith and her mother joined her in front of the bridal shop. "Sorry we're a little late. We got a late start." Faith looked pointedly at her mother, who shrugged.

"What? I wanted to get coffees for the road. You can't road trip without coffees!"

Katie laughed. "I'm glad you're turning it into an occasion."

"Of course we are! It's not every day my daughter gets married."

"No." Katie looked down. "It's not. Okay, let's do this."

"Before we do…" Faith tilted her head up by her chin. "How about a congratulations? You're done your exams, Katie! That's huge."

"How did I forget?" Her mother pulled her into a hug. "I am so proud of you, kiddo. This is turning out to be quite a summer for you."

Faith eyed her suspiciously. "You okay?"

Before Katie could answer, her mother jumped in. "You definitely have that look."

"What look?"

"The look of love." Debbie grinned. "I mean, I didn't see it at first. Probably because I was just so shocked by the whole thing. But now...well, it's *all* I can see."

Katie looked to Faith for help, but her friend assessed her with a knowing nod. "Yup," she said. "I see it."

"You do not!"

"I do," Faith continued. "A little flushed, a little dazed...I mean, not that I'm very familiar with it. But...it's there all right."

Katie dismissed her with a shake of her head. "This wedding business of yours is definitely going to your head. You don't see anything."

Faith laughed. "Just like no one saw the two of you actually ending up together? Ha. You weren't fooling anyone, Katie Langdon."

Katie did a double take. "What are you talking about?" She looked between her mother and Faith. Her mother had already told her as much, but no one else had ever said anything about Damon and her ending up together.

"Oh, for sure, Katie. The two of you were always so close, we all kind of knew something else was going on there."

"You did?"

*They did?*

She hadn't. *Had she?* Not that there was any point in denying it too much. Instead, Katie shrugged. "Well, I guess we weren't very good at hiding anything."

"Right?" Her mom linked her arm through Katie's and all but dragged her into the store. "I am *so* excited to help you with this today. I just know we're going to find the most perfect dress."

"And with your cute little body…" Faith jumped in. "I actually might need to take a few pictures of you for some promotional pictures Hope was talking about. Especially because I know we're going to find the perfect dress."

Katie felt a little like she'd just been thrown into the middle of a tornado. But, on the other hand, she was relieved to have someone else take charge of the whole process. For the next two hours, she let her mother, and Faith—who seemed to be enjoying herself a whole lot more than Katie would have guessed—and a sales attendant named Betty take charge as they pulled dress after dress off the racks, and helped her into them. Each one was more beautiful than the last, and even Katie had to admit that she was enjoying herself.

"Oh wow," Betty exclaimed, the way she did with every dress as she zipped her up. "This is…oh, wow…wait until you see this one."

Katie turned to see the tall, blonde woman with a huge grin on her face. She always looked excited, but in all the dresses that Katie had tried, the saleslady hadn't worn this particular expression.

"Are you ready to see it?"

For the first time since the whole experience had started, Katie wished there was a mirror in the change room.

"Let's go." She shrugged and let Betty lead her to the small podium with the three-way mirror in the waiting area where Faith and her mom sat.

The moment she walked in, her mom gasped and Faith jumped up from her chair. "Oh, Katie." Her mother dabbed a tissue to her face.

"Mom? Is it that bad?"

Faith shook her head slowly. "Just wait…"

Betty fluffed her skirts and gently turned her so she faced the mirror.

"Holy shit." It was probably not the most delicate thing to say, and definitely not the most appropriate. But it was the only thought that Katie could put together as she took in her own appearance.

Her eyes moved slowly down her body, taking in the entirety of what was in front of her. They'd put her in a simple, form-fitted, satin ivory dress that fell off her shoulders. It was unbearably elegant and absolutely perfect.

"Well?" Betty asked gently. "Can you picture walking down the aisle in this one?"

Katie turned a little so she could examine herself in the mirror from all angles. She'd never imagined herself in a dress quite like it, but somehow it was absolutely perfect.

"Can you see it?" Faith came to stand next to her. "Can you see yourself saying *I do* in this dress?"

Her friend's words hit her in the gut. Katie stared at herself for a moment before closing her eyes. She could *see* it. The entire moment was crystal-clear. Damon at the end of the aisle. Walking toward him. Taking his hands. *Marrying him.*

She nodded and opened her eyes. "Yes," she whispered. "I can absolutely imagine marrying Damon." She looked to Faith and then her mom, and almost started crying. "This is the dress."

It was late by the time Katie got home from the city and more than once she regretted turning down her mom's offer to grab them a hotel room so they could stay in the city. It would have been fun to spend a night drinking wine and chatting with Faith and her mom, and of course it also would have meant that she wouldn't have had to spend the last three hours driving through the mountains in the dark. But despite all the reasons she *should* have stayed, there was one big draw for her to get home.

*Damon.*

She couldn't help it, but the draw to make the drive back to Glacier Falls and the little guesthouse at ElkView was strong. *Really strong.* She'd always loved being around him, but the last few days had been different. More intense. Of course, it was because of the whole *wedding thing*.

But Katie couldn't help shake the feeling that it might be more. The kisses they'd shared had been intense in a way she would never have expected and had awoken feelings in her that no man had ever done before. It was…unsettling but also, it gave her a feeling of peace, too.

The feelings were so conflicting that if it had been anyone else, she would have laughed at the absurdity of it all. But Katie was definitely not laughing. Especially with her mom and Faith's comments about how they'd always thought she'd end up with Damon repeating through her head. Maybe she should just talk to him about it and get it out in the open. No doubt he'd laugh, and then she'd laugh, and they could go back to being friends and she wouldn't have to worry about all of these potential feelings clouding her thoughts.

The thoughts consumed her, and had the added benefit of making the drive go quickly. Before she knew it, she was punching the code into the ElkView gate and driving up to the cottage. She put the car in park next to Damon's truck and shut off the engine to sit in silence for a moment.

Katie let her mind travel back through the day she'd just had. Her last final exam. Barring any major malfunctions, she was done and she'd have her degree. Finally. But that wasn't even the most monumental part of the day. She glanced behind her at the garment bag filling her backseat. *That* had been the most monumental part of the day.

Her wedding dress.

Fake wedding or not, the dress was gorgeous and it was everything she ever could have imagined, if she'd been that kind of girl—which, admittedly, she hadn't been...until now. But it wasn't just that the dress was beautiful; it was the realization that in just a few days she was going to be marrying Damon Banks *in* that dress. And that thought didn't scare the hell out of her the way it probably should have. No, the way it *really* should have. She was getting married to her best friend as a big, giant lie and they were deceiving *everyone*. She should definitely not be excited.

*No.* Katie shook her head. She should be pretty much anything *but* excited.

She gave herself one more moment of quiet in the car to pull her thoughts together before gathering up her things, including the oversized garment bag, and heading inside. The guesthouse was dark. Damon must have gotten tired of waiting up for her. Not that she'd expected him to, but it would have been nice.

*No.* She was quick to chastise herself. She turned her key in the lock and with her arms loaded, walked straight to the couch in the dark to dump her things when the light flipped on, startling her into dropping everything in a crash on the floor.

"What the hell?" Katie spun around to see Damon standing in the small kitchen, a glass of wine in one hand, a rose in the other.

"I didn't mean to scare you." Damon's face changed, concern replacing the grin as he took in the sight of her with her purse scattered on the floor, the giant garment bag at her feet. "I'm sorry, Katie." He put the wine down and rushed over to her. "I really didn't mean to scare you. I was just going to surprise you and...shit." He looked down at her things and back up at her and for a brief moment, she thought she might cry. But then the shock wore off and she started laughing.

"You should know by now that I don't love to be surprised. Especially not after the longest day ever."

In an instant, the concern on his face vanished and he once again smiled devilishly. "And that's exactly why I wanted to surprise you with this." He held the rose out to her as if it were the prize she'd been fighting for. "Congratulations on your last exam and being finished."

She took the flower and held it to her nose. "Thank you." The shock and surprise had totally vanished, as well as the idea that she was meant to remember that this thing with Damon wasn't a real relationship. Because, in that moment, it sure as hell felt real. "That's actually really sweet of you, Damon."

"I know." He winked and bent to pick up her things. When he straightened again, he had the huge garment bag in his hand. "Is this a—"

"Wedding dress." She snatched it away from him. "And you can't see it. It's bad luck." She realized what she'd said the moment it came out of her mouth. It wasn't a real wedding, so there was no need to worry about things like luck. She turned away. "I mean…if we were worried about that type of thing. Which we're—"

"Stop." Damon put a hand on her arm and turned her back to face him. There was a question in his eyes, and more than anything, Katie wanted him to ask it. But he turned and hung the bag on the back of the bedroom door. He stared at it for a long minute before turning around again. "I'm really sorry, Katie."

"For what?" She picked up the wine and took a sip.

"For all of this. For the wedding that's not everything it should be."

"What are you talking about?" She crossed the room. "This is exactly what it's supposed to be," she said. "It's a wedding and we're going to pull it off so you can have ElkView and—"

"It's just that your first wedding should be—"

"My *first* wedding?" She couldn't help it; Katie burst out laughing. "You make it sound like I was always destined to have more than one wedding."

Damon wasn't laughing and Katie's laughter died quickly when he reached out and touched her cheek. "That's not what I meant." His finger traced her jawline and finally came to rest, cupping her face. "I just meant that I'm sorry if this isn't what you'd always dreamed about when you thought of your wedding."

"Honestly?"

"Of course."

"It isn't really what I was picturing." She shrugged. "I mean, even if it were real."

"Of course."

"But I guess I thought all of our family and friends would be there. I mean, *my* family and friends."

He winked at her and she laughed before continuing.

"And there'd be a big dance and we'd all eat." She mulled it over. It was the most honest thing she could have said, despite the confusion of feelings flooding her head and her heart. Katie's gaze flicked over his shoulder to the dress hanging in the garment bag behind him. That dress *was* everything. Her eyes once again focused on Damon, on her best friend. The best man she knew. "But all of that being said, this wedding will be *everything.*"

For a moment, Damon didn't respond. But then he leaned in and pressed his lips to hers in a warm, deep kiss that both froze her to the spot and at the same time caused every sensation within her to come alive. This was different. No one was watching. This wasn't for show. This was…*real?*

It sure as hell felt real.

Katie leaned into the kiss and deepened it. His arms came around her and held her tight as she melted into him and gave herself over to the moment. Whatever questions she had about what was going on could wait until later.

*Much later.*

---

"I really am proud of you, you know?" Damon broke the kiss, but kept his arms around her. "I think it's amazing that you went to school all on your own and now…well, it's pretty impressive."

There were so many other things he wanted to tell her, but if his brain couldn't even begin to make sense of anything, how was he going to actually verbalize it? "And I do think we should celebrate."

"Celebrate?" Her eyebrow lifted and she tilted her head in question. "Is that what we were just doing?"

"No." He shook his head. "That was just me, showing my fiancée how proud I am of her."

She grinned, but he didn't miss the flash of disappointment in her eyes as well. "Well, then…that was—" She moved to turn from his arms, but Damon spun her back and kissed her again.

This time, the kiss was deeper and more intense.

She responded with a small groan that made Damon's dick instantly hard. *Since when did Katie provoke these kinds of feelings in him?* The answer didn't matter, because the only thing that mattered was how he was feeling, right then. And judging by the way she kissed him back, she felt it too.

But then it was over.

Her lips were gone from his and she stood on the other side of the room so quickly that Damon didn't even realize what had happened for a few seconds. He blinked hard and shook his head. "What…did we…did you…what…"

Nothing coming out of his mouth made sense, but she still seemed to understand what he was trying to say.

"Maybe we should just slow down?"

"Slow down?"

She nodded. "Just…well…everything is changing so fast and with the wedding in only a few…"

"Right." *Right. The wedding.* He nodded, although his body definitely didn't agree with what his mouth was saying. "Let's slow down a little. That makes sense."

It didn't. Nothing made sense. But he nodded anyway. "We should just focus on that."

Damon turned and walked to the other side of the kitchen, needing a moment to himself. He took a breath before he turned around to face her again. "You're exactly right. But we also need to focus on the fact that you just finished your exam. And that is absolutely incredible. Oh, and I almost forgot. I planned a little surprise for you."

Katie's face lit up. "You did?"

"I did." Damon grabbed his own glass of wine and tipped it back, drinking deeply. "I spoke with Faith a few hours ago, and we've arranged some mountain biking tomorrow."

"Tomorrow? Really?"

He laughed at her surprise and poured himself some more. "I did. She called to go over a few expenses on her way home from the city and she said you seemed a little tense. I thought it would be nice to go do something fun. So…mountain biking it is."

She shook her head, but there was no mistaking the smile on her pretty face. "Was it Faith's idea?"

"Busted." He laughed. "She said something about you and her discussing it the other day. And she thought it might be—"

"So fun!" She cut him off. "It's perfect. Thank you,

Damon. I can't think of a better way to unwind and have a little fun."

He could think of a few other ways he'd like to unwind and have a little fun. But having sex with Katie would probably be a bad idea. Well…it would be a *very* good idea, but…he'd just have to settle for platonic fun with her…for now.

## Chapter Eight

THE NEXT MORNING, after yet another night of barely getting any sleep, Katie poured herself another cup of coffee and stared out the glass window. She had no idea how she was going to get through the...however many more days it would be...running on next to no sleep. But the one thing she did know was that she could not sleep when Damon was lying next to her. There was no way.

Her body was way too aware of his proximity. Especially after that kiss.

Or...all the kisses. Each one got a little more intense than the last. And even though her *brain* knew it was Damon kissing her, her *body* certainly did not. She needed to find something to distract her if she ever planned to get some sleep again.

Either that, or she would need more coffee.

Katie raised her mug to her lips and took another long drink as her cell phone rang.

Welcoming the distraction, she pressed the button to answer Faith's call. "Good morning. Please don't tell me you're cancelling mountain biking," she said as way of a greeting. "I really need the distraction."

"Good morning to you too. And no, I'm not," Faith answered. "Why do you need a distraction? Wedding stresses?"

Katie nodded even though she hadn't even thought of the actual wedding that morning. "Yup. Wedding stress," she lied. "But going for a ride will help. You ready?"

"Very ready," Faith said. "And that's why I'm calling. How many bikes do you have?"

Katie did a quick mental count of the old bikes they had in her barn. "A few for sure. Why?"

"Well, I mentioned it to Sarah. Do you remember Sarah?"

"Sarah Lewis. Of course. Don't forget, I never left this town."

"Right," Faith said. "Well, we've been hanging out a bit more lately and it turns out that there's something going on with her and Brody."

"Brody Morris? Everyone knows that." Katie laughed. Brody and Sarah were almost always together. And no matter what Sarah said about being just friends, it didn't take a genius to see that both of them wanted it to be more, if it wasn't already.

"Well, I didn't know." Faith sounded a little affronted, but then she laughed. "But I guess it makes sense."

"Exactly." Katie took another big gulp of coffee. "Hopefully they sort themselves out soon because I think it's a great thing." It was better than a great thing. Sarah had a run of terrible luck when her husband died tragically in a drowning accident. They'd been childhood sweethearts, and it had been incredibly hard on her. She'd spent the next few years completely dedicating herself to her daughter. She was a great mom with a heart of gold and she deserved so much out of life. Katie was genuinely happy for whatever it was that was going on with her and Brody, who was also a great person.

"So what does this have to do with mountain biking?"

"That's the best part," Faith said. "I heard through the

grapevine that you were hoping to start up a rental shop and offer tours and things. And…when Sarah mentioned that she'd never tried it…well, it seemed like the perfect fit. And then after I spoke to Damon last night, I had this great idea that it might be more fun with more people and—"

"Right," she interrupted, despite the fact that she'd mostly stopped listening after hearing Damon's name. It was ridiculous the way her body reacted at the mere mention of him. Again, she had to remind herself that Damon was just her friend. That was all. She was acting like a ridiculous teenager. "Sounds fun to me. And like I said, I could totally use the distraction."

"Perfect! We're all going to have so much fun."

"Who is *we all*?"

Faith laughed again. "Sarah, Brody, myself, and Damon of course." *Of course.* "Oh, and Logan," she added as an afterthought.

Katie ran her hand through her hair.

"So, this afternoon then?"

Getting out on the trails never failed to clear her head. But with Damon? *And* her big brother? This was a plan that had trouble written all over it. With a sigh, she shook her head and turned to look back at the bedroom door that Damon hadn't emerged from yet. The trails *did* seem like a good alternative to driving herself crazy with Damon's proximity. Besides, it was actually market research for the business she wanted to start now that she was done with her exams.

"This afternoon is great. We'll load up the bikes and meet you at the trail head. I'll text you directions."

---

Damon felt more than a little proud of himself for having such a great idea the day before. Sure, they probably should have been thinking about getting ready for their nuptials, but going mountain biking would be way more fun. And if he were lucky, it might take his mind off how badly he actually wanted to take his bride-to-be, push her up against the wall, and do things to her that would definitely make her blush.

Maybe if they spent a little time together doing something active and surrounded by other people, the weirdness that had been shrouding them ever since they moved into the cottage would disappear. Or at least, diminish a little bit. It was making him crazy.

Ever since they'd kissed—and then kissed again—and again—something had changed. And Damon knew Katie felt it too. How could she not? There was definitely something between them. And it was a whole lot more than friendship. It was sexual tension so thick that it threatened to consume them both if they didn't keep it in check.

*But would that really be so bad?*

That was the whole problem. Damon didn't know what could happen if they gave in to it. Was a little sexual release worth ruining their friendship? *Would* it ruin their friendship?

"This one's ready to go." Katie wheeled a mountain bike up to the truck where he'd been standing, lost in his thoughts while she prepared the old bikes they'd found in the Langdons' barn. "Can you load it up for me?"

His eyes caught hers and held them for a second. "Of course." Damon reached for the bike and his hand covered hers. She stiffened under his touch, but didn't pull away. "Katie, I—"

"If you two lovebirds are almost ready, let's get going." Logan stormed out of the barn, wheeling his own bike next to him.

Katie's mouth was open in a small O, as if she'd been caught doing something she shouldn't, and on an impulse, Damon leaned forward and placed a quick peck on her lips.

"Seriously." Logan groaned. "It's bad enough that this is all happening in the first place." He waved an arm in the air. "I really don't need to see it."

But he did. They all did. Damon knew it was selfish, and maybe he had all kinds of motives that he hadn't originally had when this whole deception began, but the more everyone saw them acting like a loved-up couple, the more everyone would believe it and maybe... He winked at Katie, who shook her head at her brother's opposition.

*Maybe they would even start to believe it themselves?*

Damon knew he was playing with fire even by letting himself think such things, but he'd been trying to fight his feelings for a few days now and it was a fight he was losing—badly. For reasons he couldn't even begin to explain, he was having feelings for Katie that were a whole lot different than just friends.

"Let's get going." He pulled himself away from Katie and hefted the last two bikes into the back of the truck before securing them and hopping down.

"Everyone else is going to meet us at the trail head. Logan, are you jumping in with us?"

Damon really hoped he would say no. Any chance he could get Katie alone when she didn't have her head stuck in a book was a bonus. But of course, Logan nodded and the next thing he knew, the three of them were crammed into the front of his truck, which, as it turned out, wasn't too bad because the length of Katie's leg was pressed up against his.

With them both wearing sport shorts, they were skin to skin, and despite the fact that it was an innocent touch, Damon's body reacted hard and fast. He forced himself not to look down at her lean, tanned thigh because he was pretty sure he wouldn't be able to keep himself from touching it. From squeezing it possessively just to feel her beneath his hand.

*Damn.*

He needed to stop thinking about Katie that way. It was only going to drive him crazy if he let himself go too far down that path. She was his best friend. That was it. She was doing him a favor. An epically huge favor, but that's all it was. A favor and he needed to remember that.

Damon did his best to concentrate on the road and the easy drive to the trail head where the others were already waiting. He kept himself busy unloading the bikes and handing out the helmets that Katie and Logan had dug up in their barn. It turned out they had what felt like an unlimited supply of bikes and gear, even if some of it was seriously outdated. Damon had looked on while Katie had given each bike a quick once-over to deem it good enough for an easy ride in the mountains. She gave out simple instructions to Sarah and Brody, who'd never ridden the trails before, and a quick refresher for Faith, who'd been living in the city too long. And the whole time he watched her, Damon couldn't help but feel a rush of warmth towards her. She was really good at explaining things in a way that was both simple but not condescending, and she clearly had a passion for it. She was going to be crazy successful with her new business venture. Of that, he was completely certain.

"Okay, if everyone is ready, let's get going." Katie stood with a helmet under her arm and looked at everyone in turn. Her gaze landed on Damon last.

He couldn't help but grin in a way that he could feel was totally goofy and ridiculous. He was proud of her and even though that felt ridiculous to admit, he couldn't help it. He was.

"Logan, why don't you lead, and I'll bring up the rear for a bit?"

"Sounds good, sis." Logan took off and everyone else fell into line behind him as Katie popped her helmet onto her head.

"Your turn," she said to Damon, who was still watching her. She did a double take. "What?"

"Nothing." He shook his head, but the grin on his face still wasn't going anywhere. "I'm just really impressed."

Her face turned a cute shade of pink as the blush crossed her face. "With what?"

"You." He knew he shouldn't, but he couldn't help it, so he reached out to clip her bike helmet under her chin. "You're a total natural at all of this. And you look damn good doing it."

Her blush deepened as Damon let his fingers linger a little. What he really wanted to do was pull her close for a kiss. A *real* kiss. One that wasn't for show, one that wasn't for anyone's benefit but theirs. Instead, he forced himself to pull back. "I guess I should get going or we'll be too far behind."

---

*What. The. Actual. Fuck?*

Katie tried to process what had just happened. Had Damon really just looked at her that way? Like he wanted to get her alone and— What did it mean? *Did* it mean anything?

No.

Of course it didn't. He'd simply told her he was proud of her. They were best friends. That's what best friends did.

*But did they kiss the way they'd been kissing?*

That was different. The kissing was different. It didn't mean anything. It was just part of the show. But she knew it wasn't. She knew what she was feeling, and more and more, it felt as though that was the way Damon was feeling, too. And was that really so bad? *Really?*

Katie continued to debate with herself as she pushed herself on the trail. They'd gotten a later start than the others and they were behind despite the fact that Sarah and Brody were beginners. Damon was riding hard and fast, and Katie had to work to keep up to him. He'd obviously remembered quite well how to handle his bike on the trails despite being gone from Glacier Falls for so long. She had no idea what he was doing to keep in shape while he'd been gone, but whatever it was, it was working.

Damon's legs were hard and defined under his shorts and when he lifted up out of his seat... *Damn...that ass.*

Not that she was looking.

Nope.

She was definitely not looking at her best friend's ass. But if she were...

"Damon!"

Katie had looked up right as Damon's front tire hit a root and he'd gone head first over the handlebars into the trees. She skidded her bike to a stop in the mud next to his and ran through the undergrowth to where he was lying flat on his back. His eyes were closed. He wasn't moving.

She'd been lucky and had never been in a bad mountain biking accident before, but she'd seen them: broken legs, plenty of fractured wrists, a few concussions, and one particularly terrible broken collarbone. It was one of the reasons she was up to date on her first-aid certification.

"Damon?" She dropped to the ground next to him, heedless of the rocks under her knees. "Can you hear me? Open your eyes, Damon." Katie reached around and pulled her backpack off her shoulders to get at her first-aid kit. Gently, she pressed her hands to his chest and then up to his neck to feel for a pulse. She leaned over him to listen for his breathing. *He had to be breathing.* "Damon, I need you to—"

His arms shot up and wrapped around her, pulling her down to him.

"I need to what?"

"What are you doing?" Katie tried to wiggle out of his grip. "You're going to hurt yourself. You need to—"

"I'm fine." He laughed beneath her and she felt the rumble of his chest under hers. "It was just a little tumble."

He still wasn't releasing her. A fact that Katie was very much aware of, just as she was very much aware of the fact that she was lying directly on top of him, their faces only inches apart. "You scared me." The words came out barely more than a whisper.

"I did?"

"Yes." Much to her mortification, tears rushed to Katie's eyes. She *had* been scared when she saw Damon fall. She'd been terrified when she'd seen him unmoving on the ground. If anything happened to him she'd—*what?*

She'd be devastated.

"Don't cry, Katie." His voice had lost its teasing tone, and while one arm remained firmly locked around her, the other hand reached up to wipe the tears from her cheek. "I'm fine. I'm sorry I scared you. I didn't mean to. Really."

She blinked hard, trying to force herself to stop crying. After all, he *was* fine. But now Damon's fingers were on her cheek. His touch was so gentle, she involuntarily leaned into it.

"I really am sorry, Katie." His words were soft, and she got the distinct impression that he was no longer talking about the bike accident. But before she could ask, his lips were on hers and they were kissing. *Really* kissing. And no one was there to watch or bear witness. There was no show. It was just the two of them.

He shifted beneath her, and Katie was able to move one arm. She brought her hand up to his and without breaking the kiss, they threaded their fingers together in an action so inti-mate, it made her stomach flutter in need.

And she wasn't the only one reacting to the kiss. Katie felt him growing hard with a need of his own. When Damon deep-ened the kiss, she groaned in response.

Damon's hand moved to her low back as he moved his kiss

to her neck. It was a warm day, but her entire body shivered as he nibbled and licked his way to her collarbone.

"Katie." Damon's voice was gruff and full of need.

There were probably a million reasons she shouldn't be doing what she was doing, but at that moment, she sure as hell couldn't think of even one. Because she'd been right—Damon *did* feel the same way. She kept her eyes closed and murmured his name in response.

But when he said her name again, it was no longer with the same gruff need. "Katie." Her eyes snapped open at the change and all she could see reflected in his was...regret. "Shit, Katie."

It only took a moment, but her heart squeezed with hurt as Damon picked her up off him and put her to the side. It was only then that she realized they weren't alone. In fact, they had an audience.

"Hey." Katie hoped she sounded natural but by the looks on the others' faces, she wasn't pulling it off. "What's up?"

"We were looking for you." Faith grinned. Next to her, Logan didn't look quite so pleased. His arms were crossed tightly, his lips pressed together.

"We didn't mean to interrupt." Brody chuckled. "And it does look like we were interrupting something."

"No," Katie answered quickly. "It's not like that. I was just—"

"I bailed." Next to her, Damon had gotten to his feet. "And Katie was just making sure I was okay."

"Is that right?" Sarah couldn't help but laugh. "Not like you need to explain it," she added. "You are getting married, after all. It's nice to see a couple so in love they can't keep their hands off each other."

Katie blushed at her friend's assessment. *If she only knew.*

But really, what *had* just happened? It's not as if Damon knew anyone would see them. *Did he?*

She wanted to look at him, but she didn't trust herself and instead busied herself with her backpack. "Well, as long as you're not really hurt, Damon."

"Are you hurt?" Sarah asked. "I am a nurse. If there's anything—"

"Honestly," Damon interrupted smoothly, "I'm fine." He touched his hand to Katie's shoulder so casually that he probably had no idea the effect it had on her. "Really, my pride is just a little hurt that I bailed in front of Katie is all."

"It's fine." She pulled away smoothly and slipped her backpack on as she walked back to her bike. "Everyone bails." She forced a lightness into her voice. "It's all part of the experience. And it makes the beers at the end of the trail even more worth it." She grabbed up her bike and swung a leg over. "How about I lead this time? Faith, Sarah, Brody—you guys fall in behind me, and Logan, you can bring up the rear." She vaguely heard Logan grunt in agreement, before she took off down the trail, eager to put some space between her and Damon and whatever had just happened between them.

## Chapter Nine

THE MINUTE she sat in the vinyl booth at the Knot, Faith could feel every one of her muscles that she hadn't used in what clearly felt like forever. She rolled her shoulders and sighed loudly. "Who knew that would be so hard?"

Sarah and Brody sat across from her while Logan went up to the bar to get them a jug of beer. Katie and Damon were suspiciously missing. Something about loading up the bikes, but Faith had her own suspicions about the couple. They'd been acting strangely all day, especially after they'd discovered them making out in the bushes. They'd gone from not being able to keep their hands off each other to barely even looking at each other. It was strange to say the least, especially for a couple about to get married.

Not that Faith had any actual idea how a real relationship worked. She'd certainly never had one. And that was exactly the way she liked it.

"That was so fun," Sarah exclaimed. She clearly wasn't as sore as Faith. Either that, or the glow of a budding relationship was clouding the aches and pains she'd likely feel later. Sarah looked to Brody, who smiled in agreement.

"That was awesome. I'd totally do that again. I never had mountains growing up in the prairies. This is way better than riding a bike through a grain field."

Faith laughed as Logan arrived with a jug of beer. It splashed over the edge and onto her hand. She shot him a look, but if he'd noticed, he didn't say anything as he slid into the booth next to her. His proximity both irritated her and...*no*. That wasn't a tingle of excitement that just flashed through her. *No way. Not Logan.*

Faith turned her attention to pouring beers and passing them around. "How long have you been in Glacier Falls, Brody?" A lot had changed in the years since Faith had moved away, including a bunch of new faces that she hadn't had a chance to get to know yet. Brody was a little different, as he owned the Birchwood restaurant and had done a bit of catering for some of the weddings at Ever After Ranch. Still, working with him hadn't meant she'd gotten to know much about him yet. And besides the fact that he seemed to be spending a lot of time with her old friend Sarah and her young daughter, she didn't know anything at all.

"I've been here just over a year now, I guess." Brody didn't seem to mind the questions. "It took me a little bit to settle in and get the restaurant set up the way I wanted it.

The Michaels had done a great job with it," he added, quickly mentioning the original owners who still lived in town, "but I had a different vision for it."

"It's fantastic."

Was it Faith's imagination, or had Sarah just *gushed*?

"Thank you." He smiled and touched Sarah's arm, letting his fingers linger. "I must admit," Brody continued, "I can't remember the last time I enjoyed cooking so much. This town and all of the residents, and of course the weddings," he pointed at Faith, who shrugged. "Everyone has been so welcoming. It makes it a lot easier to start over somewhere new."

"It's good to hear, man." Logan raised his glass. "Because we like having you and hey, maybe I've found a new riding partner?"

"What about Faith?"

Faith almost spit out the sip of beer she'd just taken. "Me?"

"You looked like you were keeping up with Logan pretty well," Sarah offered. "The two of you seem pretty evenly matched."

There was more than one thing that could be taken from that statement, and judging by the wiggle of her friend's eyebrows, Sarah knew it too. But Faith was not going in for any of that. She and Logan were just…what *were* they? Not friends. Not really. They drove each other crazy. They were co-workers more than anything and that was only because her sister and Levi had forced them together to make them feel less guilty about leaving Ever After Ranch in their hands as they went to travel the world. It was definitely not by choice.

Faith looked over at Logan and shook her head right as he said, "There's no way she could keep up with me. Not if I was really trying."

"Is that a challenge?" She turned in her seat so she faced him. Logan grinned and turned to face her as well. She tried not to notice his hard chest under the too tight T-shirt he wore or the way it stuck to his biceps. It really had been too long since she'd been with a man. She was clearly becoming delirious if she was looking at Logan in any way other than a pain in her ass.

"It could be." His voice was low and rough, and dammit if she didn't think it was sexy.

Faith shook her head and forced herself to turn away and put both hands on her beer. "Whatever. It may have been a few years, but I've still got it," she said. "Definitely not much of a challenge."

Across the table, Sarah let out a low whistle and Brody chuckled. But it was Logan's response that held her attention.

He kept his voice low, barely more than a gruff whisper, but she heard him loud and clear. "Oh, it's definitely a challenge."

The rest of the evening passed quickly over more beers and wings. But Katie and Damon never did show up to join them. Fortunately, the conversation steered away from Logan and Faith, not that there was even anything to discuss there, and after a bit, the men excused themselves to play a game of pool while the women chatted.

As soon as Faith had Sarah alone, she had to ask. "So, what exactly is going on between the two of you? Are you guys officially dating or…"

Sarah shrugged, but she wouldn't meet Faith's eyes. "Brody? Me? Oh no. It's not…we're just friends."

"Seems like more than that."

"I mean, we do spend a lot of time together. More and more over the last few months, actually. He probably spends more time at my house than his own, actually. And now that he's started coaching Rory's soccer team, well…I kind of like having him around."

Faith grinned. "So, you're dating?"

"Oh my goodness!" It was not her imagination when she saw her friend's face turn a very bright shade of pink. "No. I mean…no."

"It sure sounds like dating."

"We're friends. It's never been anything more." Sarah shrugged and looked down at the table.

"But you want it to be–"

"No!" Sarah's head shot up. "I mean….can we not talk about this anymore?"

Faith put her glass down and leaned across the table. "It's okay, Sarah."

"No." Sarah shook her head, looking flustered. "I just… we're just friends."

Faith wasn't buying it. She may not believe in love herself, but other people did. And whatever was going on with Sarah and Brody was definitely more than a friendship. Anyone could see the way they looked at each other.

"Honestly?" Sarah shrugged and turned to look as Brody made a shot to break the balls on the table before looking back at Faith. She leaned over the table and whispered, with a small smile on her face, "I really like having him around and all, but I haven't really thought about dating him. I actually haven't thought about dating anyone. I think it might be too soon."

All at once, it became clear to Faith what the problem was.

It's okay to be happy." Sarah and Josh had been high school sweethearts, and they'd all been friends in school. Faith felt certain that what she said was true. Josh *would* have wanted Sarah to move on and be happy. "And Brody is great with Rory, right? I mean, he coaches the soccer team and he doesn't even have kids. That's like next level."

She smiled. "I know, it's just…" She looked down and swallowed hard before continuing. "It's hard."

Faith smiled supportively. She couldn't even imagine just how hard it was. "Whenever you're ready, Sarah. Don't over-think things, okay? Just go with it and let it happen the way it should. And whatever you do, please do not feel bad about moving on, okay? You know as well as I do that's all Josh would want."

And she was pretty sure Josh wouldn't have any problem with Sarah being happy and moving on with Brody, but she didn't say so. Clearly her friend wasn't ready. Not yet at least.

Sarah nodded and smiled. "Thank you, Faith. It's true.

Sometimes I think I just need someone else to say it, you know?"

She did.

It wasn't until much later after Faith was home and shutting off the lights as she got ready to go up to bed that she allowed herself a moment to think. *What if she'd been wrong?* What if love *was* a real thing? She'd spent so long pushing it away and keeping any real feelings from coming close, but what if she'd made a mistake? After all, Katie and Damon had found it, even when it had been there the whole time. And Hope and Levi. And even Sarah—hell, she may have found it *twice.* Even if she didn't know it yet.

She paused in front of the fireplace and picked up a framed photo of her parents. They'd been in love. *Desperately in love,* Hope used to say. But her twin sister hadn't known the truth. She'd never known. Only Faith held onto the secret that their parents' happily ever after had all been a lie.

## Chapter Ten

BY THE TIME they'd gotten the bikes unloaded and had returned to the guesthouse at ElkView, the tension between Damon and Katie was so thick that Damon was reconsidering their decision to blow off beers with the others at the Knot. Maybe it would have been better to be around other people instead of alone with whatever it was that was going on between them. And there *was* something going on. He couldn't deny it anymore, not if he wanted to retain any sense of sanity at all. No, they were definitely going to have to address the elephant in the room. And soon.

"Do you want to shower first?" Katie asked as they walked through the front door. She moved easily through to the kitchen and opened the fridge. "I'll just—"

"No."

Katie froze with one hand on the fridge door and turned to face him. "No, you don't want to shower first?" She closed the fridge. "Okay, I'll—"

Before Damon could change his mind, he moved quickly across the space and pushed her up against the fridge. He used his arms to brace himself, but even so, the move caught her off guard.

"Damon, what are—"

He held up a finger to her lips and swallowed hard. "I think you know."

"I don't know if I—"

"No more." He cut her off. "We both know that there's something here. And really, we're about to be married, Katie."

"I'm not sure if it's a good idea…" She was trying to keep her voice light, but Damon knew her well enough to know that she was working to keep it under control. Just as he could feel her body vibrate against his.

"Katie…everything about this is a good idea." Damon pressed his mouth to hers, and in that instant, everything was right again. Every thought and emotion swirling around in his brain came into crystal-clear focus as his lips crushed hers. It took a moment, but only one—and then she was deliciously, mercifully, kissing him back.

Her arms came up, one hand holding him to her, pressed flat against his back, while her other hand ran through his thick hair. He didn't even care that they were both sweaty and covered in dirt from their ride. It didn't matter. Nothing mattered but the taste of her in his mouth.

Damon's kisses became more insistent and she groaned beneath him. *Damn, that was sexy.* The little sounds she made and —didn't even know about—made her absolutely impossible to resist. He moved his kisses to her neck, this time determined to taste more of her because there was no way they were going to be interrupted. *What would have happened earlier if the others hadn't gone back to look for them?* He certainly hoped he would find out.

"Damon." She breathed his name as he moved his kisses to the dip of her V-neck T-shirt and swell of her breasts.

He needed to see her. Touch her. *Now.*

He pulled away, but only enough to tug her shirt over her head. He tossed it to the side and sucked in a breath at the sight of her. "Damn, girl. When did you get so fucking hot?"

She laughed but then her smile faded and she looked at him seriously. "Are we doing this? Really?"

"Well, we are getting married."

"Tomorrow."

"Maybe we should wait until—"

"No."

The word came out so fast, and with so much ferocity, that Damon couldn't help but laugh.

"Point taken," he said. "And I absolutely agree. Waiting until marriage is such an outdated idea." He bent and sucked her nipple through the thin fabric of her lace bra, while his free hand tweaked the other.

She sighed, and her knees buckled a little. "It really is," Katie agreed. "So outdated."

Damon pushed the lace down over her breasts to expose them, plump and perky and so perfect the sight of her made his cock ache. "Dammit, woman. There is no way I can wait until it's official." He knew they were both playing and the wedding wasn't real, but none of that mattered. The only thing that mattered was getting Katie naked, in bed, and beneath him, screaming out in ecstasy.

Without waiting for a reply, he lifted her easily by the hips. She wrapped her legs around his waist and pressed herself into his hardness with a need that made it hard for him to focus. Somehow, Damon managed to walk the short distance into their bedroom and deposit her onto the bed.

She fell back onto the comforter and instantly leaned back on her elbows, pressing her breasts up in show. "Your turn," she said. Her eyes were hooded and having her look at him with so much desire in those pretty brown eyes almost completely undid him. Almost.

He didn't need to be asked twice. He also knew he couldn't move as slowly as he would have liked. With a few quick moves, he stripped himself of his shorts, shoes, and T-shirt, and stood before her, completely exposed.

She didn't say anything, but her eyes grew wide with appreciation. After a moment, she shook her head.

"What?"

"It's just…" She bit her bottom lip. "Well, I…I've never…I mean I have…but…"

He silenced her and the thoughts she couldn't verbalize by leaning over her, bracing his body with his arms as he kissed his way down her body, removing the rest of her clothing as he went. First her bra. Her breath caught in her throat as he sucked her nipple, now bare, into his mouth, not releasing it until her breath came hard and fast beneath him. Then he moved his kisses down her flat, toned stomach to the waistband of her shorts. He traced his fingers along the elastic before sliding them down over her hips, taking her panties with them, leaving her completely exposed to him.

It was then that Damon realized exactly what she'd been trying to say but couldn't.

They'd been friends for so long that they knew almost everything about each other. They'd seen everything.

*Almost.*

They'd never seen this. They'd never seen the other naked and completely aroused. This was new. *Very* new.

It was his turn to shake his head in wonder, but only for a moment before he dropped once more to the bed and started kissing her again, this time with nothing to come between them.

Katie's brain couldn't keep up but she wasn't sure she wanted it to. Because what was currently happening, even if it was the craziest thing ever, was a good kind of crazy.

Every time Damon kissed her body, she was sure she was going to completely combust. She wasn't sure she'd be able to handle much more, but at the same time she wanted as much as she could get, because it couldn't ever be enough.

His body was hard and lean under her hands as she explored everything about him for the first time. Part of her brain screamed at her: *This is Damon. DAMON! Your best friend.* But the other part of her brain—the louder, more insistent part —told it to shut up and enjoy.

So that's what she did. Because there was just so much to enjoy. And when his fingers slipped down her body, between her legs to tease her most sensitive spot before pressing inside her, she was no longer thinking anything at all. The orgasm ripped through her fast and strong, and she screamed out as she rode the wave of pleasure he'd created so easily in her.

When Katie opened her eyes again, Damon was watching her intently. She licked her bottom lip and smiled wickedly before reaching up and pulling him down so his mouth once again met hers in a deep kiss. She sighed into his mouth, but it wasn't enough. Before long, she wiggled beneath him until he pulled away, just a little.

"Katie, I don't have a condom." His eyes were full of regret and so much need that it made her want him even more.

"I'm on the Pill," she said without hesitation. "It's fine."

"You're sure?"

"Absolutely." To prove it, she pulled him down closer to her, and a moan escaped his lips.

Damon didn't need any more invitation, a fact that Katie was more than thankful for. He kissed her again, and right as he pushed himself inside her, she heard him say her name. But she couldn't be sure, because the only thing she could be sure of was the incredible sensations filling her body as Damon began to move inside her.

She wrapped her legs around him, to pull him in even deeper. She needed him closer somehow. Her hands clawed at his back as he pulled back just enough to look in her eyes. Katie's first response was to look away, to squeeze her eyes shut against his intensity because...*Damon.*

"Look at me, Katie." He'd read her mind. Of course he had. He knew her better than anyone. "Stay with me." His voice was rough and insistent. "Right here." His body moved slow, punctuating each word with a thrust. She did as he asked and looked straight up into the familiar eyes that were suddenly completely unfamiliar, but just as compelling.

Katie was no stranger to intimacy, although she hadn't had many partners. But nothing she'd ever experienced compared to what was happening with Damon. She forced herself to focus on his eyes, which had the effect of intensifying every other sensation through her body until finally her vision clouded as the orgasm built deep within her, starting in her core before forcing itself out in a violent full-body shudder as she came completely undone beneath him.

She was only vaguely aware of Damon taking his own release right along with her before he rolled off her to the side. It was only then she felt the loss of him and their connected-ness, but only for a second before he reached over and pulled her up onto his chest where he could hold her tight.

She snuggled into him, breathing in his once familiar scent that was now threaded with the scent of their lovemaking. It was different and for a moment, Katie's brain wanted to go to a place of panic, to a place of *what just happened.* And it might have, too, if Damon hadn't chosen that exact moment to stroke her hair and pull her tighter to him. He didn't say a word, but he didn't have to because just his presence was enough for her to breathe.

Yes, she'd just had sex with Damon. With her *best friend*. But it would be okay. It *was* okay.

Katie wasn't sure how long they laid like that, because soon her breathing matched his, and she fell into a deep, content sleep.

It was the first time since Damon arrived that Katie had slept through the night. When she finally woke, with the sun streaming through the bedroom curtains, she couldn't help but laugh at herself a little. *Was that really all she'd needed? A little sexual release to help her get a good sleep?*

Sexual release with Damon.

*Shit.*

Had she really just slept with Damon?

She squeezed her eyes shut again and pulled a pillow over her head. *No. No. No. No.*

Katie knew she was acting like a child the way she shook her head back and forth, stopping just short of pounding her heels into the mattress, but she didn't care. Because she had, in only one night, ruined *everything*. Friends couldn't sleep with each other and ever be the same again. It just didn't happen. Damon was her best friend in the whole world and now...

She screamed into the pillow, thankful for the muffling effect but needing the release regardless. When finally she'd exhausted her minor tantrum, she pulled the pillow from her face and sat up.

"Good morning."

"Shit!" Katie yelped and immediately slid back down, pulling the sheet up over her head.

She couldn't see him, but Damon chuckled and, a moment later, gently pulled the sheet away. She stared up into his smiling face. Her own face burned from the blush of embarrassment that was no doubt a bright shade of red.

"Are you done yet?"

She nodded and then shrugged. "Done what?"

"Being embarrassed." His voice was laced with humor, but it was gentle, too. He sat down on the bed next to her and waited for her to sit up. "You shouldn't be, you know?"

She didn't know. She didn't know anything. *How was she supposed to react?* This was not like any morning after she'd ever experienced or even ever imagined.

Katie pulled the sheet tight around her bare breasts. "I don't know about that," she said after a minute. "I'm not sure what happened last night. I mean…" She shook her head and corrected herself. "I *am* sure about what happened, but I don't—"

He silenced her with a kiss that was so unexpected, she dropped her grip on the sheet and it slipped down. When Damon sat back, he raised his eyebrows appreciatively. "It is a good morning."

"Dammit, Damon." She grabbed up the sheet. "That's not helping." But it was. His reaction to everything *was* helping her relax. Maybe it wasn't such a big deal after all. Maybe they could just carry on and just be them?

"I brought you coffee." He handed her the steaming mug.

"Now, that *is* helping."

"I thought it might."

She took a tentative sip and then a deeper one, letting the hot liquid fortify her. "So about what—"

"What about it?"

She stared at him. "You really don't want to talk about it?"

He shook his head. "It's not that I *don't* want to talk about it, but I don't know if it will make any difference to what I'm feeling."

"And what are you feeling?"

He took her free hand in hers. "I'm feeling like, as fucked up as this situation is, it feels right. And that feels good. Wouldn't you agree?"

She couldn't disagree. Everything they did the night before

felt good. *Very* good. And being with Damon always felt right. After a moment, she nodded. "But we're getting married today."

Saying those words out loud made it all the more real and her spine stiffened with the reality of it all.

"We are."

"That doesn't freak you out?" She stared at him. "I mean, for all different reasons than it might have a few days ago."

He laughed a little. "I'm not going to lie because of course it freaks me out. But after last night…" She blushed again and he winked. "It all feels a little bit more…real."

She nodded. *Real.* Yes. It felt real.

He must have seen the uncertainty in her eyes, because Damon's face filled with concern and he shifted closer to her on the bed. "You're okay with all this still?"

*Still? Ever? Now?*

So many things ran through her head, but as real as the wedding suddenly seemed, that wasn't a bad thing. "I am okay with it," she answered honestly. "What happened last night, it…it was great and maybe it was all just meant to be." She couldn't help but laugh at herself. "I'm not usually so *spiritual.*" She held her fingers up in air quotes. "But…well… yes. For all kinds of reasons. Let's do it. Let's get married."

## Chapter Eleven

IT WAS A PERFECT SUMMER DAY. There wasn't a cloud to be seen and the blue sky was the perfect backdrop for their nuptials. Damon took a breath and turned to look over the valley below, letting the view he loved so much fill him and bring him calm before he turned around again to look at the small gathering of family members who had collected on the decks of ElkView.

He made eye contact with Debbie, who smiled before dabbing her eyes with a tissue. His own father had a small satisfied smile on his face, as if he were pleased with himself for getting exactly what he wanted. And maybe he had. Damon was finally meeting one of his expectations and getting married. The usual aggravation that Damon would feel toward his father, just thinking about him getting what he wanted, didn't materialize. He shifted his gaze toward the cottage, where he knew Katie was getting ready to join him.

The only thing he was feeling was calm. Even the stress and tension of the last few days had vanished after the night he'd shared with Katie. He'd been a little worried about how she would react after the fact, but when she'd told him that it all felt *right*, he couldn't have agreed more. It might be a little ridiculous really, but Damon couldn't help but feel like maybe everything happened for a reason, and he and Katie were actually meant to be together.

It was crazy, but hey...crazier things had happened. And maybe, after all of this, there would be no reason to have the marriage annulled and they could just—

The music began as the door to the cottage opened and then...there she was.

She was stunning. Damon's breath caught in his throat.

Katie wore a simple, fitted dress that showed off every single one of the curves he'd had his hands all over only hours earlier. She was sexy and innocent, all at the same time. But most important was that she was walking directly toward him, her pretty pink lips curved up into the slightest smile as her eyes locked on his.

Logan held tightly to his sister's arm, but Katie didn't need any guidance as they made their way across the patio toward him. Finally, when brother and sister were standing in front of him, Damon looked away from his bride long enough to shake Logan's hand and thank him. But then when he turned and took her hands in his, he once again only had eyes for her.

Vaguely, Damon registered the justice of the peace, who was talking about love and commitment next to him. He saw Katie nod once or twice, and then it was time to exchange vows, which in their case, because they had decided to keep things as simple as possible, meant repeating after the officiant and finally saying, "I do" before she declared them husband and wife and let him kiss his new wife.

The kiss was probably not family appropriate, but Damon didn't care because more than anything, it had become crucially important to wrap his arms around his beautiful bride and kiss her senseless so that there was absolutely no mistaking how he felt about her. Not to anyone.

When he was finally able to pull himself away from her, Katie took his hand in hers and together they walked over to the table where they signed the marriage license and Faith handed them each a glass of champagne.

"Nicely done," she said. "Congratulations, you two."

"Thank you for all your work on this, Faith. I know a wedding in only a few days isn't an easy request."

She shrugged. "This was nothing. You guys made it extra easy on me. Now if you'd wanted a big blow-out with all the fancies…that might have been a little bit more."

Next to him, Damon thought he heard Katie sigh. He squeezed her hand and bent to whisper in her ear. "Are you okay?"

She nodded but her smile told him the truth. She was fine.

"You look absolutely gorgeous," he said and she smiled wider. "That dress is amazing. But as much as I like it, I'm going to like it a whole lot more on the floor when I rip it off you later."

Katie turned a sexy shade of pink, her blush reaching all the way down her deliciously exposed cleavage. But she didn't have a chance to respond to his comment because their parents chose that moment to join them in a toast.

"It was a beautiful ceremony." Debbie pulled her daughter into a hug. "And you look absolutely stunning, sweetie."

"I was just telling her that."

Katie's blush deepened and she shot him a look but she focused on her mom. "Thank you, Mom. I appreciate all your help."

"Of course."

Katie turned next to his father. "And Mr. Banks, thank you so much for your support. And for letting us use ElkView for the ceremony. It was just perfect." She gave him a kiss on the cheek, and Damon watched his father react to the attention. The smile that crossed the old man's face lit him up in a way that Damon couldn't remember seeing since his mother was alive.

"I couldn't be happier for the two of you," Anthony said. "And knowing that the two of you are going to live right here and make ElkView your home, well, it couldn't be more perfect."

"You are?" Debbie asked. "I don't know why, but I guess I thought you might live…well, I don't know. But I hadn't thought of ElkView."

"Of course, ElkView." His father turned to face Debbie. "And it worked out so perfectly since I wasn't willing to sell it to a single person. I wanted a family to buy the place ideally, but for Katie and Damon, well, I made the exception that the sale could go to a married couple."

Anyone else might have missed Debbie Langdon's reaction to his father's words, but Damon didn't, and he knew Katie hadn't either. She paused, her champagne glass almost at her lips, and she slowly put it down before looking first to Katie, then to Damon, and then finally to Anthony. "I didn't realize there was any kind of stipulation on the sale of ElkView."

Katie squeezed Damon's hand in warning, a signal he got loud and clear.

"It was just a formality." He jumped in before his father could answer. "And it worked out perfectly as far as timing went for the two of us."

Next to him, Katie beamed. "Sometimes things just work out perfectly, don't they?"

Debbie took a long sip of her champagne before looking pointedly at her daughter. "Don't they, though."

Maybe it was the champagne that had gone to her head. Or maybe she'd just gotten too wrapped up in everything. Or maybe it was because she was having genuine feelings for Damon. But whatever it was, Katie found herself genuinely enjoying her wedding celebrations. If she'd been able to plan it properly—or, of course, if it had been real—then maybe she would have wanted something a little bit bigger with all of her friends and some dancing. But she was still having fun, and everything had gone off perfectly. Katie couldn't think of a better way to celebrate a wedding.

*Unless, of course, it was real.*

She'd forced herself to stop thinking of it any other way and by the time the guests dispersed and Katie and Damon were finally alone back in their cottage, she'd almost started to believe it could be real. After all, why not? She could think of a lot of worse things than being married to Damon for real. *Especially considering the sex was…*

"Well, that went well," Damon said the moment they were alone.

"Did you think it wouldn't go well?"

Damon crossed the room and pulled her into his arms. "Not even for one moment." He kissed her then and she melted into it. "Have I told you lately how stunning you look today?"

"Not in the last few minutes." She giggled and he kissed her again.

"You do look amazing, Mrs. Banks."

*Mrs. Banks?* She pulled back and stared at him. "That sounds…"

"Good?"

She shook her head a little. "Not bad…"

"It does seem a little strange, doesn't it?" He released her and moved to the kitchen. "Wine? Or…"

"Just water for me. I think I need to clear my head a little."

Damon nodded and opened the fridge, pulling out two bottles of sparkling water. Katie watched as he poured them into glasses and rejoined her. She took the glass gratefully and drank deeply.

"Is it really that crazy?" he asked when she'd put her glass down.

"What?"

"You...me..." He gestured between them. "Being married..."

*What. Was. He. Saying?*

Katie forced herself to stay calm because she felt anything but.

"I mean, I can't think of anyone else I care about more than you," Damon continued.

She nodded in agreement. Besides her family, Damon was the most important person in her life.

"And we get along so well."

She nodded again.

"And the sex..." Damon shook his head. "Damn."

"Damn indeed."

"So, is it really that crazy?"

"To be married?" She tried to keep her voice light. "I hope not, because we are." She turned around so he wouldn't be able to see her face. No doubt she had a wild expression that was somewhere between joy and disbelief. She'd never really thought about being actually married to Damon, but now that it was happening, she had to agree with him...was it really that crazy? *No.*

Damon wrapped his arm around her and spun her to face him. "So let's say we don't worry about the annulment for a while."

"Really?"

He grinned. "I mean, it certainly seems like a shame to waste such a perfectly good marriage when we enjoy each other so much. And I think we could be really good together."

She couldn't disagree. Especially when he lowered his mouth to her neck and started kissing her right below her ear before moving his attentions down to the neckline of her gown.

"It really does seem like a shame…" Her words trailed off into a groan.

"So we're agreed then?" He spoke between kisses.

She nodded, unable to form words when the sensations he was stirring up inside her were so intense.

"Good." Damon ran his hands down her body until he knelt on the floor in front of her, the long hem of her dress gathered in his hands.

"Damon?" She tried to step backward, but came up against the living room wall. "What are you doing?"

His eyes danced with mischief. "I was going to give my new wife a little gift." He reached up under her dress with one hand and tugged at her lace panties, pulling them down. She lifted her feet reflexively, so he could take them off. "I mean," he continued, his eyes never leaving hers, "it's kind of a gift for me, too."

Katie's mind raced. *What was he doing?* She didn't do that. Or…she'd *never* done that. She'd never let anyone…not that there had been a lot of men. Only one really, and Jeremy had never… She shook her head. "No. I don't think—"

"Katie." He stopped her. "It's okay." He looked so confident, so sure of what he was doing. *But…* "Stop thinking, Katie. Really." Before she could object again, he added, "Hold this, please." He pressed the gathered-up fabric of her dress into her hands and with her panties gone, she was exposed to him.

Her body shivered, but she wasn't cold. Far from it. Damon

grinned like a cat who'd just swallowed the canary and bent forward to kiss her between the legs. But before he could, she stiffened and he stopped.

"I'm sorry," she muttered. "I just…I don't know…I—"

"Katie." He got to his feet and stood directly in front of her. He cupped her cheek with one hand, his other on her waist protectively. She could feel his warm breath on her face as he spoke. "Do you trust me?"

Without hesitation, she nodded. "Of course."

His smile was slow and sexy as it crossed his face. "Then you need to trust me now, okay?"

Damon waited for her answer and when she finally bit her bottom lip and nodded, he kissed her quickly on the lips and once more got to his knees in front of her.

---

It was insane for Damon to think that Katie had never been kissed in such an intimate way before. How could any man be with her, and not want to taste how deliciously sweet she was most certainly going to be? The thought boggled, but at the same time, the idea of her being with anybody but him made him a little crazy. So as soon as the image came into his head, he pushed it away so he could focus on the task at hand.

And what a task it was.

With one hand holding the thin cotton of her dress out of the way, he sat for a moment and admired the beauty of her. But only for a moment, before he leaned forward and with more restraint than he thought possible, kissed his new wife softly in her sensitive center.

She let out a low moan in response and her knees quivered just slightly.

*Oh, I'll make them weak, baby.*

Encouraged, he kissed her again, only this time he ran his tongue down her seam and she cried out.

*Damn. To hell with restraint.*

He began licking and kissing her most sensitive spot in earnest. She tasted so incredibly sweet and her response was absolutely perfect. The noises coming from above as she tried, and failed, to control herself only excited him more. He'd been looking forward to this moment all afternoon, imagining how it would be to have his mouth on her, his tongue inside her, driving her higher and higher until finally—

"Oh my God, Damon!"

Katie's body shuddered and her knees threatened to collapse as he focused his attentions, driving her further and further to the point of no return, until finally it was there and her orgasm hit her.

She cried out and after a moment, Damon sat back on his heels to look up at her face. Her eyes were squeezed shut and he found himself wishing he could see them, and the way they darkened when she was consumed with pleasure.

He waited, and after a moment, her eyelids fluttered open and she looked down to where he sat.

"Um...I..."

"You don't have to say anything." He grinned and got to his feet so he could pull her close. She nuzzled her face into his neck and Damon breathed in the scent of her. He held her until finally she came back down to earth and pulled away just enough to look up at him.

"That was..." She shook her head with a smile. "Pretty freaking amazing."

"I can't believe you've never...damn, those men weren't worthy of you, Katie." He pressed a kiss to the top of her head.

"Not *those* men. Just one."

Damon stiffened. They'd never had the *how many partners*

*have you had* talk. Even as best friends, that was one area they never discussed and Damon knew exactly why. *Jealousy.* He hated to admit it, but it was true. He'd been jealous of Jeremy when they were kids, and now…it was him again. The only other man who'd had the honor of laying his hands on Katie. And even though he had absolutely no right to it, the idea of that consumed Damon with jealousy.

He forced himself to take a deep breath and focused on the exhale before he said, "Well, he's a fucking idiot." Before she could respond, he added, "But that doesn't matter anymore."

And it didn't. He needed to remember that. She was *his* wife. Not Jeremy's. She'd said yes to him. Even if it hadn't been real at first, it was real now. At least it would be real. It *could* be. And the fact that they were on the same page together made him genuinely happy.

He ran a hand down her back and held her a little closer. "Today was perfect. Wasn't it?"

"It was beautiful."

They moved to the couch with their glasses of sparkling water. Damon couldn't wait to get her into their bed, but there would be plenty of time for that. And plenty of time for him to introduce her to all kinds of pleasure.

"I really am sorry if it wasn't the type of wedding that you've always dreamed of."

Katie tucked her legs up under her on the couch. She had such a beautiful post-pleasure glow about her, it made her even more gorgeous. "I meant it when I said it was beautiful."

"But…"

She grinned. He knew her too well. "But," she looked at him pointedly, "I think if there had been different circumstances, I would have liked a big dance and all our friends and family."

"Really? A big white wedding?" He sat back and crossed

one leg over the other. "I don't know if I would have guessed that."

"I'm full of surprises, Banks. Just you wait."

They both laughed but after a moment, her laughter faded. "Do you think my mom...well, did you see her face?"

He had, of course, but had been hoping that Katie didn't notice. "I'm sure she just thinks it's a coincidence that we got married at the same time as the house sale."

"I hope so. I would hate her to think...well..."

There was no need for either of them to finish the sentence. "Don't worry about it, okay?" He reached out and squeezed her hand. "Tell me more about the wedding that you *would* have had."

Katie laughed again. "I really haven't thought about it that much. But it would have been nice to have a first dance and maybe a father-daughter—"

Tears filled her eyes and her hand flew to her mouth as she realized what she'd been about to say.

"Katie, I'm so sorry your dad wasn't here." Damon put his glass down on the table and moved so he could gather her into his arms. "He would have been so proud of you. You just finished your degree and now...you're a remarkable woman, Katie, and I'm sure he would have given anything to be here today."

She was silent for a moment, letting the emotion run its course, and he didn't push her as the tears rolled down her cheeks. Finally, she sniffed loudly and wiped at her tears. "I'm sorry, Damon. I don't know what came over me."

"I do." He tried a small smile. "It's still new, Katie. It's okay." It *was* still new. Her father had only passed away a few months ago and she'd just gotten married without him giving her away. Of course, she hadn't been worried about it before, because it was all meant to be fake. Just the way he'd thought about his mother more than once throughout the day. She would have loved to know that he was marrying Katie. Damon hadn't given it much thought before, but now that there were real feelings involved…it was different.

And just as he couldn't have imagined a few days ago that there might be some very real feelings involved with a marriage that wasn't ever supposed to be real, now, he couldn't seem to imagine it any other way.

## Chapter Twelve

DAMON TOOK the trail that led from the cottage and away from the main house, avoiding it the way he had since he'd moved in. It was ridiculous, he knew that, especially now that he was actually married to Katie and they'd pulled it off. Not that he was even thinking of it that way anymore. Not really. It had been two days since they'd said their vows, and as crazy as it all was, it felt a little more real every day.

There really was no reason to avoid the main house, or his father. Not anymore.

Even so, Damon continued on the trail that led him to the hills, and farther away from his dad.

Before turning the corner that would take him out of view, Damon glanced back toward the guesthouse at the thought of Katie. He knew she was inside, writing out plans for her new store, and he couldn't help but be impressed by her drive and dedication. She was so excited about the opportunity, and that excitement was contagious. He knew he'd been distracting her from her plans, but as long as he was in close proximity, he couldn't seem to help himself.

Once he'd had a taste of her, he couldn't seem to get

enough. Katie was like a drug he'd never known he'd needed. And just like any drug, there was a very real danger of becoming addicted. He just needed to be careful, that was all. Because as much as he was enjoying himself with her—and he was—he needed to make sure he kept things in perspective. Not that he really knew what that perspective was anymore. They'd discussed the idea of actually *staying* married and he hadn't really thought she'd agree, but when she did...well... maybe giving in to his addiction for her wasn't such a bad idea after all.

They'd stayed mostly holed up in their cottage for the last few days, and they'd been some of the happiest days Damon had had in a really long time. Marrying Katie might just have been the best decision he'd ever made. Although, despite the lightness that came with the newness of a relationship, there was still a small part of him that couldn't shut out the reality of the situation and the nagging feeling that he'd actually ruined things between them because he'd pushed for more. After all, wasn't it historically a bad idea to sleep with your best friend?

*Only if it didn't work out.*

His inner dialogue just wouldn't shut up.

Damon focused on the view of the valley below. It never failed to calm him. He picked his way along the pathway that had become overgrown since the last time he'd taken it. Which, admittedly, must have been years ago. His dad likely didn't come out this way. He'd never been much of an outdoorsman, preferring to enjoy the view from inside looking out. And now, with his health and the nursing care he needed—*for what?*—a flicker of guilt snapped through him. He hadn't actually asked his dad how his health was. He hadn't asked his dad much of anything. Not that they'd ever been big at communicating. But still, Damon should have tried harder. Reluctantly, he looked toward the house and decided to stop in on his way back from his walk.

His relationship with his dad might be hard, but that didn't mean he had to be a total asshole about it. He shook his head in acceptance before continuing down the trail.

It had been his mother who'd been the one to venture outside with him. She'd shown him the beauty of the mountains and the trails that crisscrossed them. Together, they'd hiked up to the glaciers and along the river. She'd taken him on long drives on the back roads so they could *explore.* And explore they did. They'd found countless treasures hidden in the mountains, from an icy-cold, tiny, but impossibly deep lake surrounded by cliffs that they could jump off into the frigid water below, to the spectacular waterfalls that only happened in the spring with the runoff from the mountains as the snow melted down into the valley. Damon had loved those days with his mom. And then when he got older, he'd shown his friends all the places they'd found. Mostly.

He remembered the last time he'd wanted to take Katie to a particularly beautiful spot. They never got there because she'd insisted on bringing Jeremy along, so at the last minute Damon had pretended that he'd forgotten where he really wanted to go. But the truth was that he couldn't imagine sharing the special hot springs with anyone except Katie. And definitely not the boy she was dating. Or worse, could be in love with.

The thought of Katie being in love with Jeremy stopped him short. *Had they been in love in high school?* He hadn't thought so. Not really, but then again, they'd dated recently. *Very* recently, if Jeremy's outburst on Main Street had been an indication of anything. Katie had said it was nothing, just a casual thing. But still.

*Was that really all there was between them? And did he have any right to even ask about it?*

Damon shook his head and took a deep breath. He was getting himself worked up for nothing. He really needed to keep things in perspective. He found a boulder and perched himself on top before digging his cell phone out of his pocket and pressing the numbers for his buddy, Nick.

"Hey," Nick answered. "Are you back in town yet? Or still roughing it in the woods?"

Nick's generally dismissive attitude about Damon's hometown was always a bit of a burr in his side, but for the most part, Damon tried to ignore it. He'd met Nick at college and he'd been part of the team he'd worked with on the microchip, which meant that Nick was just as wealthy as he was, a fact that had been both a good and a bad thing in their relationship. It was hard to find real friends when you had a lot of money, but on the other hand, sometimes that money could change people. In Nick's case, it had turned him into a bit of a playboy-party animal, a role Damon had joined him in for a little bit, which was why it was extra-hard for him to understand why Damon would choose to move back to his hometown.

"I wouldn't call it roughing it." Damon looked around at his surroundings. No, definitely not roughing it. "I'm actually calling because I have news."

"News? Like you're coming back to the city next week? Because there's a party at—"

"No." He cut him off. "Nothing like that. I'm actually calling because I got married." Damon waited, sure that there would be a reaction.

Sure enough, Nick started to laugh. "Married? You? Like, now?"

"Like two days ago."

"You're not kidding."

"I'm not."

"Well, shit."

"Shit indeed." Damon smiled. "And I want you to meet her."

"Your wife?"

*Wife.* The word sounded so good. Damon nodded. "I do." He wanted everyone to know Katie was his wife.

There was a silence on the other end for a few minutes, and then Nick said, "Okay then. When should I come?"

---

Faith looked around the barn, full of happy wedding guests, celebrating and dancing and generally having an amazing time. It was Saturday night and the room full of people had no idea that the woman who'd just pulled off the wedding they were enjoying so much barely even knew what she was doing, and only a few weeks ago would have panicked at the very thought of being in charge of such a thing.

A feeling a little like pride flowed through her as she stood in the door of the kitchen and watched. Hell, if she had time, she might even laugh at herself and the whole idea that she was in charge of a wedding business. Because even after the last month, it still struck her as hilarious. But that didn't matter, because whether she believed in the whole thing or not, it turned out that she was actually pretty good at it. After all, she'd pulled off Katie and Damon's big day, small as it was, all by herself.

Faith's eyes scanned the room and landed on Logan, who was carefully trying to extricate himself from a wedding guest who'd clearly had a little too much to drink and was trying to get Logan to dance with her. As if he could sense her watching him, Logan looked up and met her eyes across the room with an unspoken plea.

She couldn't help but chuckle. But despite the fact that he pushed all of her buttons, she couldn't bring herself to leave him in the situation. In truth, he'd actually been quite helpful with not only this wedding, which had gone off perfectly so far, but with pretty much all of them since Hope and Levi left.

Except maybe his sister's. Ultimately, he'd shown up to give her away, which was arguably the best thing he could have done. So, even though he'd been pretty adamant about not being involved, he wasn't as stubborn as he would have led her to believe.

So technically, maybe Faith kind of owed him. Besides, he hadn't been so bad lately.

Faith tucked her clipboard onto a shelf just inside the kitchen door, straightened her pencil skirt and, with a slight shake of her head, crossed the room to help Logan out of his predicament.

"Come on." The wedding guest, a cute brunette with a very low-cut gold dress, tugged on Logan's arm as Faith walked up. "Just one dance. You won't get in trouble."

"Oh, but he will," Faith said smoothly. Not missing a beat, she slid her hand over Logan's back and pulled him into her. "Because he's my boyfriend, and I have this weird jealousy about him dancing with other women. I'm sure you understand." She spoke as sweetly as she could, with a gentle smile to the other woman, who clearly wasn't used to being turned down.

Almost immediately, the woman dropped her hands from Logan's arm and crossed them over her chest. "You didn't say you had a girlfriend." She stuck her chin up in defiance.

Logan gave both women an apologetic look, but it wasn't enough for the spurned woman.

"How long have the two of you been together then?"

Faith was not ready for a challenge. She shook her head, ready to tell the guest exactly what she thought about her advances on Logan. Either that, or leave the man to figure his own way out of the situation that no doubt he'd had some part in. Faith knew enough about Logan to know that he was a merciless flirt, although she also knew he'd never mess with a guest, no matter how cute she was, or how low-cut her dress was.

"It's still pretty new," Logan answered smoothly right as Faith was about to say something that no doubt would have gotten her in trouble. "We're still trying to figure a few things out."

To her surprise, he pulled her close to him and draped his arm heavy over her shoulders. It was the last thing she wanted, but a completely unexpected shot of desire went through her at his touch.

Well, maybe it wasn't *completely* unexpected. Or really unexpected at all. A little more every day, her annoyance with Logan was turning into something a little bit more, despite the fervor she'd used to tell herself otherwise.

The woman seemed to accept that as enough of an explanation, and with a final humph in their direction, she turned and somewhat unsteadily walked away to find someone else to get out on the dance floor.

"It's pretty new, is it?" Faith turned but Logan didn't remove his arm; he simply let it slide around her as she moved, so they were still in a sort of embrace.

"Hey," he said with a small grin, his gaze fixed steadily on hers. "You're the one who called me your *boyfriend,* which is funny because I didn't think you went in for that kind of thing."

"Boyfriends?" She shook her head. "I don't."

"Hmmm."

"What does that mean?"

Logan brought his other hand up and brushed a strand of hair off her face, tucking it behind her ear. The move was so unexpected and intimate, that Faith immediately stiffened.

"Hey." Logan's voice was low, a little intense, and something about it sparked another shot of desire deep in her gut. "I don't bite, you know."

She couldn't help it; Faith giggled. She *giggled*.

*What the actual fuck?*

Whatever was going on, it needed to stop, *now*. Before it went *any* further. Because even though there were some serious waves of want rolling through her at that exact moment, and he smelled *really* good and it had been awhile since she'd—no! This was Logan. Mr. Drives-her-crazy—annoys-the-crap-out-of-her—makes-her-stabby, Logan Langdon. This was not someone she could entertain, not even for a one single second, anything more than friendship. And even that was suspect.

Faith was so busy debating with herself that she hadn't realized that Logan's hand now cupped her cheek and some-how, they moved even closer together, until he whispered, his breath hot on her lips, "But I can do this."

And then his lips were on hers.

And they were hot and soft and moving just right against hers.

And not only did she not want to push him away, she wanted him closer.

Faith knew she shouldn't be kissing Logan for so many reasons, not the least of which was the fact that they were in the middle of an event. An event that she was responsible for, and making out, even if it was in a dark corner, was completely unprofessional. But despite that logical part of her brain telling her to stop before things got even further out of control, she pressed her body closer to his and groaned into his mouth.

Logan responded by pressing his hand to her back until they were so close there was a real risk that they were going to become one, and deepening the kiss. She could feel every part of him pressed up against the softness of her own body, and there was no doubt that he wanted it just as bad as she did. Maybe more.

The idea excited her, and for a moment, she almost completely lost herself in her own lust.

"Damn, Faith." Logan broke the kiss to whisper roughly in her ear. "Let's get out of here. I need to get you alone."

*Yes.* Her body was screaming yes in a million ways. She was the type of woman who'd always been in firm control of her sexuality. She knew what she wanted and when she wanted it. And wanting what she wanted had nothing to do with a relationship. Logan was perfect.

Except…

*Dammit.*

Faith put both hands on his chest and pushed him a little so he was still close but no longer pushed up against her, affecting her ability to think straight. She shook her head and touched her fingers to her lips. "No," she said. "We can't do this."

"And why not?" Logan bristled. "Because from what I could tell, you wanted to do it just as much as I did."

*Maybe more.* But she didn't say it out loud.

"Because we're working," she hissed. "We can't act like some randy teenagers at the back of the barn in the middle of a wedding." Faith moved to look at her clipboard and realized she'd left it in the kitchen. "We have to get set up for the bouquet toss right away and the garter. We can't just—"

She was interrupted by his hand around her wrist. Logan pulled her close again with a quick tug. Her body still vibrated with the need he'd stirred up in her, and more than anything, she wanted to give in to his kisses and forget the wedding completely. He kissed her hard and fast, sucking her bottom lip between his teeth as he pulled away. "Okay," he said when he released her. "But this isn't over."

She took a step back, needing to pull herself together.

Logan licked his lips and watched her as she straightened her blouse and skirt, an outfit designed to blend in and be professional. "No," he said slowly, the desire sparking in his eyes. "This is far from over."

## Chapter Thirteen

KATIE HAD NEVER BEEN a vain person. She'd never given her clothing choices a second thought, something that had irritated her mother on more than one occasion over the years. Like when she'd shown up for her parents' anniversary dinner wearing jeans and a plaid shirt. She'd been running late, and had come straight from the barns, where she'd been shoveling fresh hay into the horses' stalls. At least she'd put a clean shirt on over her T-shirt. But she had definitely not expected her mom to get so angry. And then there was graduation, when she'd completely forgotten to buy a dress and had gone down to the local thrift store to find anything that would fit. It hadn't been a total disaster, though, because she'd lucked out with a simple black sheath dress that had actually looked quite glamourous.

It wasn't that she didn't care; it was more that she didn't think it was important to spend her time worried about what she was wearing.

Which was why it was so strange that she'd developed some sort of paralysis when it came to picking out an outfit just to go to the pub with Damon.

But it wasn't *just* a trip to the pub. Not really. It was their first official outing as a married couple and even though that shouldn't feel weird or that it was a big deal—it did.

Maybe more so because in the last few days since their wedding, everything had changed.

It was so much more than a game to get ElkView. It was way more than a deal to get the startup capital for the Hub. Things between Damon and her were…real. Well, mostly real. They hadn't actually discussed their relationship beyond that one time after they exchanged vows, but something between them had definitely shifted. And it wasn't just the sex. Although the sex was pretty damn amazing.

Things with Damon felt both easy and complicated at the same time. They'd largely spent the last few days hidden away from everyone, having what they called a *honeymoon*, alone in the cottage. But Katie couldn't shake the feeling that they'd been hiding. If they weren't around other people, it would be easier to believe that their wedding had been real. And maybe their feelings as well. *Would it be different around other people?*

She didn't know what to expect. Everything was starting to feel more and more out of control. Katie had hoped that a few days' distance from the actual wedding would give her clarity, and a way to justify what they'd done and the giant lie that she'd been telling everyone she cared about.

Of course, now with the lines between fact and fiction blurred even more, things had only become more confusing. And easier than trying to figure it out had been for her to stick her head in the sand by immersing herself into a business plan for the Hub, the store she wanted to open as soon as possible. If everything went according to plan, she might even be able to close on the space she'd found on Main Street in a day or two. Damon was handling the purchase negotiations at the same time as the paperwork for ElkView.

The same flicker of guilt that she felt every time she

thought about how she'd gotten the capital to open her store flashed through her body. And just as she always did, she pushed it away. After all, did it really matter *how* she got the money, as long as no one was getting hurt? And no one was getting hurt.

*Except maybe you.*

The thought slammed into her so hard, Katie took a step back and plopped on the edge of the bed.

Only a week ago, Katie would have felt very differently. The plan had been a marriage of convenience. Nothing more. No feelings beyond friendship. Sex had a way of changing things.

But it wasn't just the sex, and she knew it.

*No one is going to get hurt.*

She squeezed her eyes as she repeated the thought to herself one more time, willing herself to believe it. But no matter what she told herself, Katie could not help but shake the ominous feeling that had taken hold.

"You look nice."

Her eyes flew open when Damon walked into the room.

"Sorry." He gave her a kiss on the cheek. "Did I interrupt something?"

Katie forced a smile to her face and stood. She glanced in the mirror at her simple white sundress. She hadn't intended it to look so bridal, but she was out of time to change.

"Nothing at all," she said with a brightness she wasn't sure she felt. "Are you ready to go?"

---

"Cheers to the happy couple." Sarah raised a glass in yet another toast and everyone followed suit. They clinked glasses and drank deeply once again.

"I don't know if we need to keep doing that." Katie shook

her head and pushed her glass away. "I'm out. Someone needs to drive home."

Under the table, Damon slipped his hand over her thigh and squeezed gently. She offered him a smile, but it didn't quite reach her eyes. She'd been acting a little off all night, and Damon couldn't quite put his finger on what was going on with her. She seemed to be having fun, but whenever the conversation turned to their recent nuptials, she got quiet.

As if to prove his point, Sarah, who'd had a few drinks, tried again to discuss it. "I wish I could have seen you in your dress, Katie. I bet you looked stunning."

"She did." Faith jumped in. "In fact, I totally should have gotten more pictures. I can't believe I didn't. I mean—"

"You were a little busy." Katie shrugged. "But it wasn't a big deal, Sarah. I'm sure someone has a picture."

Damon could tell she was trying to blow it off and change the subject, but the other woman was not taking the hint.

"Didn't you want a bigger party?" she asked. "I mean, I'm not going to lie, it sounds very romantic that there were only a few of you there, but the whole first dance and the cake and—"

"Not really."

It was a lie and Damon knew it.

"What about you?" Damon turned the questioning around, to get the attention off Katie. "Would you ever want the big wedding again?" He realized the moment the question came out of his mouth that it probably wasn't a good one.

Sarah got quiet and sat back in her seat with a small shake of her head.

"The wedding we had last Saturday was a huge one." Faith jumped in, clearly able to read the mood of the room. She shot Damon a look. "Everyone came from the city and they were a total party group." Faith started to regale the table with tales of drunk guests coming on to Logan and after a few minutes, everyone seemed to have forgotten about the awkwardness.

Damon snuck a look at Katie, and even though she looked to be smiling and laughing, she still seemed quite distracted.

"Hey," he whispered into her ear. "Want to—"

"I just need to go to the bathroom." She interrupted him. "Excuse me for a minute?"

"Of course."

Damon stood and pulled her chair out for her while she grabbed her purse and made her escape to the ladies' room.

He watched her go for a moment and then turned to his friends. "I'll grab another round. Be right back."

The moment he was at the bar, he gestured for the bartender, ordered a round, and an additional shot of whisky for himself. It was supposed to have been a fun night, but he couldn't help but wish he and Katie were back in the cottage, tucked away from reality, alone from the outside world again. Things had seemed a lot simpler then. *Maybe she was second-guessing their decision to stay married? Was she regretting her choice?* Damned if he knew. She wasn't talking.

Damon took the shot the moment the bartender poured it and downed it in an easy swallow. He gestured for another.

"Shots, huh?" a voice behind him said, followed by a slap on the back. "I'll take one, too."

Damon turned to face the voice and immediately broke out into a massive smile. "Nick." He hugged his buddy, clapping him on his back. "You made it. Thank God."

"Is it that bad?" Nick turned to survey the room. "I mean, it's a small town, but I'm impressed. This place is packed."

"It is. I'm glad you made it. You were supposed to text when you got in. I would have met you."

Nick laughed. "I'm a big boy. And meeting at a bar seemed pretty perfect to me."

The bartender slid two glasses of whisky toward them and they clinked glasses in a mini toast.

"I am glad to see you, though. It's been stranger than I thought, coming back to town after so long."

"Strange how?"

Damon sipped, rather than shoot his whisky this time, and contemplated telling Nick the truth that he hadn't even told Katie—that he'd expected life in Glacier Falls to freeze in time when he left. He'd expected to come back and have everything be exactly how he'd left things. But his friends had moved on. So many of them had moved completely, and the ones who had stayed, their lives had all changed. He couldn't help but think of Jeremy. And Jeremy with Katie. He didn't want to, and he'd been doing his best to *not* think of Jeremy with Katie, especially considering their own relationship had progressed.

But he couldn't help it. *That* was definitely one thing that had changed since he'd left. They obviously had a relationship of some kind, and no matter what Katie had said, Damon couldn't shake the feeling that there'd been more to whatever had gone on between them than Katie had said. *Had he interrupted something between them when he came to town? Had Katie settled by staying with Damon? Was it Jeremy she really wanted but she'd felt forced into a relationship with him because of their deal?*

He didn't want to think about it. And he was definitely not going to ask her about it. That certainly hadn't gone well the last time he'd tried.

"Hello? Damon? Did I lose you there for a minute?" Nick stared at him with a half-smile. "The only thing strange here is you. Maybe you've been back in this place too long."

Damon didn't like the way Nick said *this place*, but he didn't bother to say anything.

"Strange like, nothing stays the same."

Nick nodded. "That's true." He raised his glass and drank what was likely whisky, deeply. "Just like you moving off to some backwoods town to marry the local sweetheart and leaving me high and dry."

"Hey." Damon spun to face him. There was nothing distinctly offensive about the way he'd referred to Katie, but it was definitely implied. Or did he just *think* it was implied?

"I don't mean any offense." Nick held up his hands. "I'm just saying, we had a good thing going in the city. Bars, women, parties, more women." Nick grinned and lifted his drink in a silent cheers. "It's been a good run."

"It has." Damon agreed, but he didn't see it the same way Nick did. Not really. Sure, he'd enjoyed the party lifestyle for a while. Who wouldn't? They were young and had money to burn. It was every young man's dream come true.

At least for a little while.

After a few months of waking up next to a different woman every Sunday morning, Damon had started to get tired. Tired of pretending he was something he wasn't. Tired of the women he was picking up, taking out on the town, and sleeping with. Tired of pretending that they were something that they weren't. It's not that they weren't nice women. Maybe they were. But they weren't the *right* woman.

His eyes traveled across the room to land on Katie, who'd reappeared from the washroom.

They weren't Katie.

*Was she the right woman?*

It was a ridiculous question, and if he hadn't been standing with Nick, he might have laughed out loud at himself. Katie was *Katie*.

She was a fabulous woman. *And she was his wife.*

He shook his head clear of the thoughts and the questions that he shouldn't even be asking himself. "But that time is over now," he said to Nick. "I'm all settled down now."

Damon tipped his glass back and drank the rest of the

amber liquid in one swallow. The alcohol was starting to dull the edges a little and relax him.

He reached backward to tap on the bar. He needed another drink.

"Well, I can't say I'm super excited for you, man." Nick shook his head. "But if that's your new wife, she's pretty damn hot."

Jealousy, anger, and something else he couldn't pinpoint flared up inside him at Nick's words. But as soon as the feeling rose, he squashed it. Nick was his friend. Possibly his *best* friend with the exception of Katie. She'd been part of his life for so long that he couldn't imagine her *not* being there. And maybe that was what was bothering him. If this whole marriage of convenience thing blew up... *No.* His eyes settled on her, dressed in a gauzy white sundress, looking absolutely gorgeous, and he knew in an instant—he'd be destroyed if she ever turned her back on him. He didn't know how he'd live through one day on earth if Katie wasn't there. Maybe he never should have crossed that line with her and put their entire relationship in jeopardy. But he had. *They* had. So the one thing he did know was, no matter what, it was all going to work out. It *had* to. There was no back-up plan.

"That *is* Katie, right?" Damon was jarred back into the moment with Nick's question. "Because if she's your wife, she sure looks pretty close with that guy." He followed his friend's gaze and it didn't take long to see what Nick was referring to.

Damon's blood ran hot. Blood pounded in his ears and for a moment he had trouble seeing straight.

That *was* Katie.

And Nick was right. She did look pretty close to that guy. To *Jeremy.* With his arms on either side of her, blocking her in as if he were having an intense conversation. He couldn't see Katie's face, but he could see the way Jeremy leaned in toward her. He could see the proximity that the other man stood to her. He could see him with her. And she wasn't trying to get away.

"Fuck." He muttered under his breath, but Nick heard and chuckled with a shake of his head.

"Looks like you have your work cut out for you. A firecracker, is she?"

Damon's vision clouded and any hope in hell that he had for keeping his jealousy in check went straight out the window as Jeremy leaned in to *kiss* his *wife*.

---

"What are you doing?" Katie squirmed out of Jeremy's arms, just a little because he was standing too close to get away completely. But enough to stop his lips from touching hers, which seemed to be the most pressing matter. His arms caged her in against the wall. "Jeremy," she hissed. "I'm *married*."

"No."

He pulled away enough to look in her eyes. They were full of hurt, and Katie felt a rush of sympathy for him. But also a rush of anger. *What exactly did he think he was doing?*

"This is crazy, Katie. This…whatever it is."

"It's a wedding, Jeremy. *My* wedding. Well, not today but…" Katie tripped over her words, flustered by his presence or his words, or both. She didn't know. "A few days ago, Jeremy. You can't do this. I'm married to Damon." She tried to look over his shoulder to see whether Damon was nearby. She both wanted him to see what was happening so he could put a stop to it, and at the same time, she desperately hoped he hadn't seen anything because the last thing she wanted was to make a scene or have Damon misconstrue anything.

"You need to talk to me about this, Katie." Before she could object to what he was saying, Jeremy grabbed her hand

and pulled her through a door into the kitchen. "You need to help me understand."

As soon as they were alone, or at least out of sight from their friends, Katie spun to face him. "Understand what?" He'd clearly had a few drinks, but Jeremy had never been the type of guy to drink much. In all the years they'd been friends and dated, Katie had never seen him drunk. "You can't do this, Jeremy. I'm with Damon."

He laughed. Jeremy took a step back from her, dropped his head back and laughed. It was so unexpected that, at first, Katie didn't know how to react. She stood and watched as humorless laughter overtook him. When Jeremy showed no signs of stopping, Katie turned to leave and rejoin the party. The very last thing she needed was to deal with this. Not now.

"Stop." The laughter cut off abruptly. "Don't go."

Katie froze in place but didn't turn around.

"Katie, please." Jeremy's voice dropped. "You need to explain this to me because I just don't understand how this happened."

He sounded so sad and confused that Katie's heart broke a little bit. She hadn't led him on. Not really. And definitely not intentionally. But they hadn't been dating. They'd been… "Jeremy." She reached out to touch his arm. "I'm sorry if this is confusing for you or if it's unexpected—"

"Unexpected?" He pulled back and gave her such a harsh look that it hurt her heart a little bit. "I'd say it's unexpected, Katie. You've known Damon for how long?"

She shrugged. It wasn't a question she needed to answer.

"And for all that time, were you ever interested in him? Like even a little bit?"

She couldn't answer that. Not honestly. Because the truth was that there had been a few times in the past where she'd considered the idea of Damon as more than a friend. Truthfully, they'd been short-lived and definitely nothing that stuck around as a real thought, but still…there had been times. But if she told Jeremy that, it would hurt him even more and that was the last thing she wanted.

"This is…" He ran his hands through his hair and turned in a slow circle before stopping in front of her. "Is it because of the money?"

Her back stiffened. "Pardon me?"

"It is, isn't it?" He nodded, as if he'd figured everything out. "I mean, I get it. He's richer than…well, he's richer than anyone I know. I get how that would be appealing. I get how—"

"Screw you, Jeremy." She pulled her arm back, ready to slap him into silence. *How dare he insult her in that way.*

But before she could make contact with his cheek, Jeremy's hand clasped down on her wrist and he pulled her close so she was pressed up against his body. His arms wrapped around her tightly and a second later, his lips were on hers.

The kiss was messy and hard and not at all welcomed. Katie squirmed in his grip and was just about to bite down on his tongue when it was over.

"I'm sorry." Jeremy sobbed and dropped his head onto her shoulder.

It took Katie a second to realize that he was crying. Actually crying. Her bare shoulder was wet with his tears as he released his emotions. Confused and not really sure how to react to his outburst of completely confusing emotions, she brought her hands up to his back and patted it in a way she hoped was comforting. "Jeremy, I don't really know what to tell you…"

"It's okay, Katie." He shook his head but didn't lift it. "I mean, no, it's not okay. None of this is okay. I thought we had something. I thought that maybe you just needed a little bit of time and then we'd be able to take it to the next level. I didn't think that…well, shit, I didn't think that you'd marry Damon. It's just such a…"

Finally, he lifted his head and looked at her. Tears streamed down his cheek and the sight of him, his heart breaking right in front of her, caused tears to well up in her own eyes.

*Were things more serious with Jeremy than she'd thought?* Seeing the pain in his eyes caused Katie to question everything. *Had she broken his heart? Had she misread everything?*

*No.* She knew in her heart that she hadn't misread anything. She wasn't wrong. They were casual. They'd always been. They'd even discussed it and together they'd agreed that they were never going to be anything more to each other than a casual thing.

Katie cleared her throat and tried again. "Jeremy, honestly, I didn't think we were like that. We discussed it, right? I mean…well, anyway, I'm sorry if I misread it, but I don't have feelings like that for you. I'm married to Damon. I need you to understand that."

He nodded, but she could see that he didn't understand. Not really. And he still hadn't released her from his grip.

Katie moved to slip away but he held her fast. And before she could move away, he kissed her again.

This time there was more urgency behind his kiss, as if he could change the past with the sheer power of his lips. There was nowhere for Katie to go—Jeremy had her pinned.

Vaguely, she heard the kitchen door swing open, the noise of the crowd out in the bar filling the kitchen for a moment and then, "What the actual fuck?"

*Damon!*

*Shit.*

With one last effort, Katie managed to get her hands between them and she shoved Jeremy away from her right as Damon grabbed his shoulder and whirled him around.

Jeremy took a stumbling step backward; his hand touched his lips as if he couldn't even believe he'd just kissed her. And then Jeremy's face shifted as he looked at Damon. Jeremy held up his hands and took a step backward. "It's not what you think—"

"Really? Because it looks like you were kissing my wife."

"I…we…Damon…"

"Damon!" Katie stepped forward to grab his arm, but the look on her husband's face stopped her.

"I should have known, Katie." His eyes were narrowed and he looked at her with such disgust it hit her directly in the gut.

"What?" Shocked, she shook her head. "No. You don't—"

"I see how it is."

"No! You don't see anything." Was he really upset with *her?*

Damon shook his head and moved to leave. "I'll just go."

"Damon!" She grabbed his arm but he shook it off and stormed out of the kitchen.

Her entire body shook as she spun to face Jeremy. "What the actual fuck, Jeremy?" She'd tried to be nice, she'd tried to talk to him and put herself in his shoes, but enough was enough. "You don't have to like it," Katie continued, trying but failing to control her voice. "But you are going to have to accept it. I'm married to Damon." She took a step toward Jeremy, her hand shaking as she pointed at him. "And if you ever touch me without my permission again, you will regret it. Do I make myself clear?"

She didn't wait for a response, but turned and fled the kitchen. She was furious and hurt and so completely confused. But those feelings were going to have to wait. First, she needed to find her husband.

## Chapter Fourteen

DAMON only vaguely heard his friends, and Nick, who no doubt was even more confused than the rest of them, call out as he pushed his way through the crowd and out into the parking lot. He pulled his truck keys out of his pocket and immediately shoved them back in. He'd had way too much to drink to get behind the wheel.

*Fuck.*

He looked around—for what, he didn't know. But he had to get out of there before—

"Damon!"

*Shit.*

Katie was both the only person, and the last person, he wanted to see.

"You're not driving."

She stormed across the parking lot and put herself between him and the truck. Her face was flushed and with her breath coming in short bursts and her hands on her hips, Damon couldn't help but think about how sexy she looked, despite the fact that she looked royally pissed off.

*And guilty?*

He was a little too far over the line of intoxicated to tell the difference. But she *should* feel guilty. After all, he had just found her getting cozy with another man.

"I know, Katie. I'm not going to—"

"Here." She held out her hand for the truck keys. "I'll drive."

Damon glanced behind him at the bar, but neither of them had any intention of going back inside. That much was clear.

He gave her the keys and walked past her to the passenger side door.

The drive back to ElkView was quiet and tense, the air between them full of everything they probably should have been saying to each other.

He looked out the window and watched the dark landscape pass by in a blur, questioning his choices.

*Why had he wanted to come back to Glacier Falls in the first place? Did he make a mistake? Was marrying Katie a mistake? Or was it falling in love with her that had been the mistake?*

Love.

The word hit him in the gut. *Did he really love her? Like, love her love her?*

Was that why he was acting like such an idiot?

It was. He knew it.

Seeing her with another man…it was too much. It had brought out a reaction in him that he couldn't even begin to explain, let alone contain. Was that love?

Maybe not. But everything else…that *was* love. He knew it. He *felt* it.

*Didn't he?*

And even if he did…what about her? Did Katie love *him?*

He knew the answer to that, too.

*No.*

His head swirled with the combination of the questions

and the alcohol that flowed through him. He wasn't the type of man to give up. He never gave up on what he wanted.

Damon glanced over at Katie behind the wheel of his truck.

*Why should it be any different now?*

He wanted Katie, and he'd be damned if he was going to give up that easily.

---

He'd had too much to drink. That was clear.

She needed to talk to him and clear up what had just happened back there. She risked a glance over at him in the passenger seat. Damon stared out the window, a hard line set on his mouth, his forehead wrinkled as if he were in deep thought. And maybe he was. But he was also drunk.

Katie shook her head and focused on the road. She needed to talk to him, desperately. But there was no point in bringing anything up in his condition.

Nothing good would come from that.

Instead, Katie pressed her own lips into a hard line and tried to ignore the tension between them as she drove them home in silence.

The best thing they could do was just get to bed, so Damon could sleep off whatever he'd had to drink and maybe Katie would have a chance to process the swirl of feelings that more and more were consuming her thoughts.

"Okay, Damon." She finally spoke as she unlocked the front door. "I think maybe if—"

He cut her off by wrapping his arm around her waist and pulling her in through the door into the cottage.

"What are you doing?"

He pressed her up against the wall and it was clear to both of them exactly what he was doing. Her body reacted immediately to him, an instinctual response, but she could smell the whisky on his breath. It reminded her of what had happened and exactly why it was a better idea just to go to bed.

"You know what I'm doing." He leaned in and breathed heavy against her mouth.

Katie shook her head and turned away. "Damon, I think you should—"

"Kiss you?" He moved to kiss her, but at the last minute, she dodged him.

Katie worked hard to keep her voice neutral and non-confrontational. "You're drunk, Damon. You need to—"

"What I need is to kiss my wife." His voice held an edge, but still his eyes danced with mischief, as if he'd forgotten that they'd just had a blow-out in the kitchen of the neighborhood pub.

And she was definitely *not* going to kiss him. Not now. Not like this.

"No," Katie said gently. "You really need to go to bed."

Damon took a step back and assessed her. "I don't," he said after a moment. "It's actually the last thing I need to do." He shook his head and walked into the small kitchen. He grabbed a half-drunk bottle of wine they'd corked a few nights earlier. "Have a drink with me? I think we should talk."

"I'm really not in the mood."

He ignored her and poured out two glasses, sloshing some of the red onto the floor. "Here." He thrust a glass in her direction a moment later. "Just a sip. Besides, don't you think you owe me?"

She grabbed the glass before it spilled everywhere and glared at him. "Owe you? What is it exactly that you think I *owe* you for?"

Damon drank deeply from his own glass before putting it down hard on the table. "You kissed another man, Katie. That's adultery."

He slurred on the last word and Katie clenched her teeth together.

She shook her head and put the glass down next to his. "You're an asshole and an idiot."

"I may be the idiot." Damon stopped her with his words before she could leave. "But you're the asshole, Katie."

Her whole body shook, but she didn't bother replying. With an exhale, she turned away.

"At least I was honest."

His words slapped her across the back and almost took her out at her knees. Slowly, she turned. "What?" Her voice was incredulous, barely more than a whisper. "You were what?"

"I was honest, Katie." Damon crossed his arms over his chest. "And that's more than I can say for you."

"What are you talking about?" It was ridiculous trying to have a conversation with him, she knew that, but she also knew that alcohol could loosen the tongue, and she needed to know what was going through his head.

"If you were in love with another man, you never should have agreed to marry me." His words slurred again. "Or at the very least, you never should have agreed to *stay* married to me."

"I'm not in—"

"Because I meant it, you know?" He took a step around the table toward her.

"Meant what?" Logically, Katie knew she shouldn't listen to whatever he was saying, but she couldn't help herself. She needed to know how he really felt. "What did you mean?"

"I meant it when I said that I thought we could be good together." He stood so close to her, she could feel the heat of his breath with his every exhale.

Katie released the breath she was holding. *Good together.* It wasn't until he actually said the words that Katie realized what she'd been hoping he'd say. Sure, they were *good together.* And they always would be. But was she naive to think it could be more? That it could be love? She'd been foolish.

"Right." She nodded and bit her lower lip. She would not lose control of her emotions. Not over this.

"We're good together." He said it again, but this time it sounded more as though he were trying to convince himself.

She shook her head sadly. "No, we're not."

He looked at her for a moment, his eyes searching hers for something. "We are, Katie," he said finally. "Tell me you don't feel it, too."

What was she supposed to say? That she didn't think that they were good together, but they were *amazing* together? And that ever since he'd come back to Glacier Falls, she'd finally felt more at home in her hometown than she'd ever felt? Was she supposed to say that it was more than being *good together?* It was about the overwhelming, full-body feeling that she was completely and totally in love with him and that she was terrified that her heart was about to shatter because it all became crystal-clear in the worst way?

No. She couldn't tell him any of that. Not like this.

Katie shook her head, a move Damon interpreted to mean something very different. She saw it the moment that it happened, the moment he registered in his own mind how she felt. Or at least, how he assumed she felt.

Damon's eyes darkened, his face hardened, and he dropped his hand from her arm. "Okay." His voice was clipped and controlled, stripped of emotion. "I get it. Message received loud and clear."

"Damon, I didn't say anything. I—"

"You didn't have to. I got it, Katie. This is business. An arrangement."

*No. It wasn't. It wasn't like that at all. At least not for her.*

"Damon, don't do this."

He held up a hand to stop her protests. "I'll tell you what,

Katie. The papers are almost signed. Give me a few days. Two tops." He held up his fingers. "You can get your money, start your little shop, and go back to your *lover.* Judging by what I saw earlier, you're counting the days yourself before you can—"

"Fuck you, Damon." She slapped him then before he could say anything more. Her palm stung from the contact but she curled her fingers inward both to hold in the heat and stop herself from doing it again. He didn't deserve that kind of attention.

Instead, she turned on her heel and, with her heart breaking with every step, walked out without another word.

## Chapter Fifteen

IT WAS EARLY on Thursday as Faith made her way down Main Street and into the Birchwood restaurant for her meeting with Brody. The overcast morning had the rain clouds looking as if they could spill at any moment. Faith breathed in the fresh air but she wasn't worried about rain. At least not the way she would be if there were a wedding at Ever After Ranch that weekend. It was still hilarious to her that she was so in tune with the weather forecast now.

But it didn't matter whether it snowed on Saturday, because she had the weekend off and she planned to enjoy every minute of not thinking about flowers, or wedding cakes, or first dances, or any of it. But she couldn't start relaxing yet. The weekend was a few days away and she still had a to-do list a mile long, including some details for a promotional campaign she'd been working on, and one last meeting with Brody for an upcoming event.

At least she didn't have to worry about what was going on at the barn. She'd left Logan in charge of that.

*Logan.*

She surprised herself by blushing just at the thought of Logan.

*Blushing.*

Faith didn't blush.

Except for maybe the night before at the Knot when he slid his hand across the booth to her leg. No one else had seen it, and it hadn't gone further than a quick squeeze of her thigh. Just enough to get her attention. And maybe that had been the point. After Damon and Katie had rushed out in a flurry of what could be described as drama, Damon's friend Nick had introduced himself and joined them at the table.

He was attractive, a fact that hadn't been lost on Faith. But despite how good-looking the newcomer was, her attention was still on Logan. A fact that she'd found more than a little troubling. And despite trying *not* to think about it, it was all she could focus on.

"So, this is what I have." Brody dropped a file on the table in front of her, startling her in the present, and away from thoughts of Logan.

Probably a good thing.

No. *Definitely* a good thing. She didn't need to be thinking of Logan in any way.

"All I need from you is a final head count next week, and let me know if we have any allergies I should be aware of."

Faith flipped open her binder to the file for the Glick and Hunter wedding for the following week.

It hadn't been long that she'd been in charge of Ever After, but much to her surprise, and just a little dismay, she was getting pretty good at the wedding planning business. Never in a million years did she think that would happen. Never mind the idea she had for a little social media marketing. Hope would be so impressed.

For the next few minutes, they discussed final numbers and

ironed out the last few details for catering. Brody's files matched her numbers, just as she knew they would.

"So, do you have any exciting plans for the weekend?" Faith shut her binder, the meeting over. "With no wedding to organize, I myself plan on doing a lot of sleeping."

Brody laughed. "If by exciting you mean coaching a soccer game before eating burnt burgers, then yes. Very exciting."

"That does sound exciting." It didn't. At least not for Faith, but Brody looked pleased.

"So things are getting pretty serious with you two then?"

Her friend shrugged but his smile dipped a little.

"It's not?"

"No," he said quickly. "We're just friends."

*Friends.* There was that word again. Maybe the two of them couldn't see what everyone else clearly could. She nodded as if she understood, which she most certainly did not. She didn't know the first thing about a relationship, having avoided them for her entire life. *So far.*

She shook her head to clear that random thought. The very last thing she planned to do at this stage in her life was change her entire belief system regarding love because of Logan Langdon. Not in a million years. The idea was so crazy, it was almost laughable. They hadn't even had sex.

Not that sex was any basis for a relationship.

"What about you?"

The question took her off guard. "What about me?"

"You and Logan—what's going on there?" Brody's question was innocent enough. At least, it should have been. There's no way he could know what it might stir up. "I hear you're not much for the *love* thing."

*Okay, maybe he did know what it would stir up.*

Faith shook her head. "I see people have been talking." She raised an eyebrow, but he only shrugged.

"Just Sarah. She mentioned that it was a bit of a worry

for your sister, Hope, and that you've never really bought into all of this." He used one arm to encompass the two of them and no doubt all the wedding stuff in general. "She also said that to her knowledge, you've never had a boyfriend."

"That's not…okay, I guess that's true."

Brody smiled kindly. "What's that all about? You're a beautiful, successful woman. I would think that you'd have men knocking down the door." He nodded and leaned back in his chair. "Hell, you probably do, don't you? But it's not for a lack of choice, is it?"

"What is this, a therapy session?" She laughed in an effort to hide her discomfort, but it did nothing to alleviate the uncomfortable sensation building within her. "It's just not ever something I've been interested in."

*Until now. Maybe.*

The little voice in the back of her head chimed in the way it was doing more than she'd like lately. *Was it because of Logan?* Never before had she entertained the idea of a real relationship. Except maybe with Noah. She had liked Noah. A lot. *Could it have been more with him?*

She shook her head and forced a light smile to her face. Because it didn't matter whether it *could* have been more or not. The fact of the matter was that it wasn't more and it never would be.

But as much as she'd like to believe that was true, deep down, she wasn't sure she believed that particular story she'd been telling herself any longer.

"Besides," she said to change the subject. "I thought we were talking about you and Sarah?"

"Sorry to pry." Brody laughed. "I just…well, I guess it's one of those things, you know?"

"I don't."

"It's just so funny that you and your identical twin, raised

completely the same way, are so different in this one fundamental way."

"I don't know if it's funny." She crossed her arms as she
tried, and failed, for levity. "Or fundamental."

"You don't think love is fundamental?"

She shook her head.

The very last thing she wanted to be doing was having this
conversation and she itched with discomfort. She hadn't even
told the people closest to her about that day when she was
fifteen and had overheard the conversation that had changed
everything for her. Not even her parents knew that she'd heard
them talking that sunny afternoon. That she'd heard the argument, heard the hurtful words they'd tossed back and forth so
casually instead of handling them with care like the daggers,
with the power to destroy lives, that they were.

Even now, so many years later, she could still close her eyes
and be right back there, in the stairwell of their home, with her
parents on the porch. Her mother crying while her father just
yelled at her, accusing her of—

"Faith?" She opened her eyes and Brody was watching her,
concern lining his face. "Are you okay? I didn't mean to…well,
I'm sorry if I said anything to upset you."

"You didn't." She forced a smile again and tried to chuckle,
but the memory was too vivid, too clear, and she knew it fell
flat.

"Okay." He didn't believe her and it was easy to see why
when he passed her a box of tissues. She hadn't even known
she was crying.

## Chapter Sixteen

DAMON'S HEAD pounded and the handful of painkillers he'd taken that morning had done very little to touch it. He thought about taking more, but didn't bother. He deserved the pain. Hell, he deserved a lot more than a headache. He welcomed it as penance to his behavior from the night before.

His hand reached up to touch his cheek where Katie had slapped him. The mark was long gone. But the sting of it remained. He almost wished it had left a mark. It would have served as a visual reminder of what an asshole he'd been.

Damon almost never drank as much as he had the night before. And there was a reason for it. Alcohol had a tendency to loosen his tongue and it made him say things that he didn't mean.

Like most of what he'd said to Katie the night before.

*Most.*

Because he'd also said a lot of things he'd meant.

*Maybe he should have said more?*

Damon squeezed his eyes shut and shook his head, causing a fresh round of pain to shoot through his temple. *Good.* He needed to remember how, in just one night, he'd let his jealousy and insecurities ruin everything he had with her. Or could have.

Because after all, they were *good together.*

Drunk or not, Damon remembered very clearly the look on Katie's face when he'd said that. Of course it had been true. He *did* think they were good together, but more than anything, he thought a whole lot more than that. It went way beyond just functioning well as a partnership. *Way* beyond that. He loved her. He was absolutely sure of it. And maybe love was making him act like an ass. Not that it was an excuse, but…an explanation?

It wasn't good enough.

Damon rubbed at his face and tried once more to focus on the papers in front of him. The real estate contract from his father. His lawyers had sent them over for final review. All he had to do was sign them.

But he couldn't bring himself to do it.

He pushed the papers away and pulled out another envelope. The loan documents for Katie's store. They'd also arrived the day before. But instead of telling Katie, he'd tucked them away. Also unwilling to sign them.

Both documents represented everything that was wrong about their relationship. And that was bullshit, because there was way more good about them than wrong. There always had been.

Katie had stormed out the night before. It had been the first night he'd spent away from her in just over a week, yet it felt like a lifetime. How could he not remember at all what an empty bed felt like?

If it hadn't been for the alcohol, Damon never would have slept at all. It was a small mercy, really.

Just for good measure, Katie had taken his truck keys with her when she left. It had probably been a good idea, because no doubt he would have tried to go after her, despite the state he was in. He assumed she'd gone to her mother's. An assumption that was confirmed when Logan showed up with his truck keys about an hour earlier. Thankfully, he hadn't said anything to indicate that Katie had told him about their fight. That was a good sign, right?

*A sign of what?*

That she was keeping their secret as promised? Or maybe, and more likely, that he'd screwed up more than even he thought he had.

Oh yeah, he'd definitely screwed things up. Damon pushed away from the desk and the papers. He walked to the window and looked out at the gray day. He was a smart man. Some might even say a genius. But genius or not, he could be pretty friggin' stupid. He put his hand straight on the glass in front of him and leaned in.

He refused to believe that it was over. Not like that. Not from a drunk night. And definitely not if he had a say in it.

An idea began to formulate as his mind cleared from the drunken fuzz. He moved toward the desk and the paperwork scattered there that only a few days ago had felt like the most important thing in the world. But he'd been wrong. Katie was the only thing that mattered.

And he was going to prove it.

With a deep inhale, Damon nodded, his decision made, and gathered up the papers. He took one last look at the view —*his* view—before making his way down the path to the main house…and his father.

---

It felt as if Katie had only just fallen asleep when the sun began to peek through the curtains of her bedroom.

Her childhood bedroom at home on the ranch.

She stretched her arms over her head and felt the pull in

her muscles. And for one brief moment, she managed to forget.

It was just an ordinary day, waking up in her ordinary house. Just like every other day.

Except it wasn't.

There was nothing ordinary about her days lately.

And after that fight with Damon, there was definitely not going to be anything even remotely ordinary about this day either.

Reluctantly, Katie forced herself out of bed and made her way into the kitchen, where her mother was taking a tray of muffins from the oven.

"Good morning, sweetie."

"That smells delicious."

"They just need to cool." Her mother smiled, but there was an unasked question in her eyes and Katie knew she was dying to know why her newlywed daughter was currently waking up in her childhood bedroom. "Help yourself to coffee. Sugar's on the table."

Katie poured herself a steaming mug and took it to the table, where she sat in her usual chair. She contemplated how much to tell her mother about why she was really there. Was there even a point in keeping up the facade anymore? Clearly, she and Damon weren't going to go through with the whole "staying married" thing. It was probably a stupid idea in the first place. She never should have married him. *That* had been the first bad idea, of course, followed by so many others. But none of them had been nearly as bad as believing even for a second that he could actually love her. Like, love her love her.

She dropped her head into her hands.

"So?" Debbie put the muffins on the table and it was the combination of the delicious aroma and her mother's question that made Katie lift her head.

"Blueberry?" She ignored her mother's question and

reached for a muffin. It was too hot, so she dropped it back on the plate and put her fingers to her lips.

Her mother raised an eyebrow. "They need to cool, so you might as well tell me what's been going on."

Katie looked into her mother's eyes and that's when she knew that her mother's question went deeper than requesting an explanation for why she had slept at home.

"I don't know what to say."

"The truth, Katie." Her mother's voice was soft, and without judgment. "Always the truth. And just start at the beginning, okay?" Her smile was kind and encouraging as she poured cream from the pottery creamer jug Katie had made in the fifth grade into her coffee.

Katie nodded. *The truth.* She could do that.

So she did.

Slowly, and carefully, Katie told her mother everything, starting with the phone call from Damon asking for the favor, to the meeting with Anthony Banks that pushed up the wedding, to the kiss and the…well, she left out specific details, but her mom got the gist. Katie spoke about the wedding, and the feelings she actually felt for him. The love that she didn't even know she'd had for her best friend, so that when they decided to actually *stay* married, it had felt like the exact perfect thing. And finally, she ended her story by telling her mother about their fight the night before that had resulted in her storming out.

When she was finished speaking, she finally reached for a muffin and pulled a chunk from it to stuff in her mouth.

A flash of movement from the corner of her eye distracted her, and Katie turned just in time to see Logan's back in the hallway before she heard the slam of the front door.

*Had he heard her? Did it even matter if he had?*

Katie shook her head, resigned, and turned back to her mom, who still hadn't spoken.

Her mom was quiet for so long that Katie wondered whether she'd heard anything she'd just said. Finally, she looked up to see her mom with tears in her eyes.

"Oh, Mom. Please don't cry." Katie dropped the muffin. "I'm so sorry for lying to you and everyone else."

"I knew," her mother said slowly.

"You knew?"

"Well, I knew something was up," Debbie explained. "After the wedding, when Anthony mentioned ElkView and selling it to a married couple."

*Of course.*

"It all just made a little more sense, you know?"

Katie nodded. "I know it was a terrible thing to do and wrong for so many reasons but Damon really wanted ElkView and Mr. Banks wasn't being reasonable about it at all and then he told me he'd give me the money to start up the Hub." The moment the words were out of her mouth, she realized how terrible they sounded. "I mean, that's not *why* I did it. I mean, Damon would have loaned me the money anyway, but…oh God. Everyone is going to think I'm a gold digger."

Being home was supposed to make her feel better. But maybe that just wasn't an option right now.

"Is that the real problem?" Her mother's tears had stopped and she sat perfectly still, staring across the table at her daughter. "You're worried about what everyone will think?"

Katie didn't even have to think about the question. *No.* That was far from the real problem. She shook her head.

"I didn't think so." She was silent for a moment before she asked, "Tell me what the real problem is, Katie. Why are you really upset?"

Katie took a deep breath and let it fill her completely before exhaling. "I love him," she said simply. "I don't even think I realized it, but I'm completely in love with him."

Slowly, her mom's face changed and a smile stretched across her features. "I know you do."

"You do?"

Debbie laughed. "Do you remember when only a few days ago I was telling you that I've known for years?"

Slowly, Katie nodded.

"I'm not going to pretend that what you both did was okay. Because it wasn't." Her mother's face hardened for a moment. "But I also don't think anything I can say will punish you any more than the hurt you're going through right now." She took a thoughtful sip of her coffee. "What I don't understand is why you finally realizing how much you love Damon is a problem?"

Katie didn't know whether it was her mother's understanding, the restless sleep she'd had the night before, the question itself, or just the buildup of emotion that had finally hit a boiling point, but tears began to pour unchecked from her eyes as she gave in to a snotty, snorting, ugly cry. Her mom waited patiently for her to get control of herself and finally when Katie trusted herself enough to speak again, she told her the simple truth. "He doesn't love me back. Not like that. You were wrong, Mom. We weren't ever meant to be."

---

Damon found his father in the living room at ElkView, just as he knew he would. He stopped in the entry of the living room and stared out the huge picture window at the view and everything he was about to give up. But as much as he loved it, it was nothing compared to what he'd already lost when Katie walked out.

"Are you going to stand there all day? Come in already." His dad's rough voice interrupted his thoughts.

Damon looked down at the papers in his hand. ElkView was already his.

But it was all based on a lie.

A lie that had effectively destroyed everything that really mattered.

With a sigh, Damon stepped inside the room. "I have to tell you something, Dad." He moved through the room until he stood next to his father, who hadn't yet looked away from the view.

"Isn't it something?" his dad asked, as if Damon hadn't spoken. "There's just no place like it, is there?"

Damon shook his head. "There's really not."

"I know you love it here as much as I do, Damon. Maybe more. I'm glad that you're going to raise your family here."

The guilt washed over him fresh. "About that, Dad. I need to—"

"I was wrong, Damon."

"Pardon?" He stared at his dad, openmouthed. He'd never once heard his father admit to being wrong. "About what?"

"ElkView always should have been yours." He still hadn't looked at Damon. "I was wrong to offer it for sale. I..." His voice cracked and his head drooped.

Damon shifted from foot to foot. Was his father *crying?* He didn't know what to say, so instead he waited for his father to compose himself.

After a moment, Anthony cleared his throat awkwardly and continued. "Your mother would have been so angry at me for keeping ElkView from you."

"You didn't, Dad. I'm going to..." His words trailed away and he looked at the papers in his hand that would have officially made ElkView his.

"But I did, Damon." Finally, his father turned to him. Damon had never seen such sadness in his father's eyes. Not since his mother died. "I put the restrictions on the purchase because I knew you wouldn't be able to meet them."

His dad's confession hit him in the gut. *He'd actively tried to keep his childhood home from him?*

But was he really surprised? He'd always known that was his dad's plan, hadn't he?

Damon shook his head slowly but before he could ask, his dad spoke again.

"I'm sorry, Damon. It was wrong."

"But why?" He ignored the apology. "Why would you do that? This is my home."

Anthony nodded slowly. "It is. And like I said, it was wrong. I never should have done what I did. I was just so…" When he looked up, his eyes shone with unshed tears. Damon had never seen his dad cry. Ever. "I think on some level, I wanted to punish you because she loved you more."

Damon took a step backward as the words hit him. "What?" He shook his head, completely unable to process what his father had just said. "Who? Mom?"

Anthony nodded but still, there was nothing but sadness on his face. "I don't expect you to understand this, son. I barely understand it myself. And maybe it's old age that's finally helped me realize what I should have seen all along. Coming face-to-face with death will do that to you, you know? You start to look at things differently."

"You're not dying, Dad."

"I am." His father let his lips flicker up into a slight smile. "But that's not what this is about." He cleared his throat with a wet, rattling cough. "I never forgave you for being her favorite."

"I was her son."

"Before you came along," he continued as if Damon hadn't spoken, "oh, the way she would look at me. As if I held the moon for her. I've never been loved like that. Not before, and not after." He looked down at his lap for a moment. "And when you came along, it all changed. And for years, it didn't matter. We were a happy family. Envied by everyone who knew us. But when you got a little older, that's when I noticed. I could never compete with what she felt for you."

"Again," Damon repeated himself, "I was her *son*. You weren't supposed to compete with me."

"I know." Anthony nodded slowly. "I know that now. But I was too immature, too jealous, too headstrong, too...well, I was a lot of things, Damon. But I was *not* a good father. And because of that, I failed as a husband. She never said anything, never told me I wasn't enough. But I could see it in her eyes when I would turn you away. And for that, I hate myself. Not only for the years I lost with you, and for all the ways you didn't have a father you could depend on, but also for the way I failed the love of my life.

"I am deeply regretful, Damon. And it wasn't until I saw you with Katie that I truly understood the depth of what I'd done."

"Katie?" The reason he was there jerked him back into the reality of his present predicament. "What does this have to do with Katie?"

For the first time, his father's smile reached his eyes. "With the two of you, I see true love. The type your mother and I shared. A deep bond that can hardly even be explained because of the intensity of which you feel it in your heart."

"Dad, I have to tell you something." It was time to end this. Past time. He needed to come clean. "I should have—"

"If I hadn't been so goddamned angry years ago, I'm sure I would have seen it then," he continued, not hearing Damon. "Your love for Katie, that's the real deal, my son. Anyone can see it. And I couldn't be happier for you. And that's why I'm giving you ElkView." Anthony laughed a little, but it quickly turned into a deep cough.

Damon moved closer and handed his dad the cup of water

that sat on the table next to him. He waited patiently until his dad regained his composure.

"What do you mean, you're *giving* me ElkView?"

"I'm doing what I should have done in the first place. This is your home, Damon. There is no one who deserves this place more than you do. And I know you have the money to buy it. Hell, you have the money to buy ten of these places. But that's not the point."

His dad reached out, and Damon took his hand in his. It felt light and papery, as though it might break if he squeezed too hard.

"This is your home. And now it's yours. I had my lawyers draw up new paperwork earlier today. Tear that up." He gestured to the papers Damon still held. "I want you and Katie to raise your own family here. It's my gift to you both."

"But you said—"

"Forget what I said." He pulled his hand away. "Like it or not, it's done. As of eight o'clock this morning."

*ElkView was his? Just like that?*

Damon could hardly believe what his dad was saying to him.

He looked straight into Damon's eyes and a tear finally slipped down his age-spotted cheek. Suddenly, his dad looked much older than his years. "I'm sorry, son. I hope you can forgive me."

Guilt flooded through Damon. It was all too much. He sank into the chair in front of his dad, heavy with the truth. "I hope you can forgive *me*," he said. "Dad, I need to tell you something. Katie and I...well, it's not what it looks like. I asked her to—"

"I already know what you're going to say."

"There's no way you could." Damon shook his head.

"Do you think I'm stupid, son? Do you think I was as successful as I was in business by trusting blindly in what people told me? Or do you think that maybe I did a little bit of research on my own?"

Damon sat back and assessed his father, who continued to talk.

"I know you and Katie weren't a real couple."

"You did?"

Anthony chuckled, but it turned into another cough. When he finally composed himself, he continued. "Of course I did. But I also saw that it was what the two of you finally needed to realize your own feelings after all this time." He shook his head in wonder. "Two more stubborn and clueless people as to what is right in front of them, I've never met."

"But...we—you let us go through with the wedding..."

"Like I said, son. Sometimes people need a little nudge."

*It was a nudge, all right.*

"But now Katie and I...well...we're not really..."

"You'll fix it." Anthony raised his arm to signal his nurse. "A love like yours doesn't come along every day." He nodded. "Yes, you'll fix it. And then you'll live here and raise your family."

Damon watched in silence as his father's nurse collected him and started to wheel him out of the room. Before he left, Damon stood and called after him. "Dad?" The nurse turned him so Anthony could look at his son. "Thank you."

It was gratitude for so much more than ElkView, and they both knew it.

## Chapter Seventeen

FAITH FELT like she was on a mini-vacation. After her meeting with Brody earlier, she'd been certain that she'd return to the ranch to see that Logan hadn't taken care of even half of her to-do list. She'd been wrong.

He'd not only taken care of her list, but even a few other things that she hadn't thought to ask him about. If she wasn't so perpetually irritated by him, she might have even considered thanking him. Of course, he wasn't anywhere to be found.

Now, as much as she thought she would enjoy the little break from work, Faith couldn't help but feel bored. She'd tried to busy herself around the house and had spent the rest of her morning lingering over coffee and cleaning the already spotless kitchen. Now, with the rest of the day ahead of her, she couldn't think of a thing to do.

She sat down hard at the kitchen table again and picked at the corner of a placemat before reaching for her cell phone.

*You up?*

. . .

She typed the simple message to her sister and waited. Seconds later, the phone rang.

"Oh good," Faith said into the receiver. "You're up."

"It's five in the afternoon here." Hope laughed. "And I'm not much of a napper, so yes, I'm up. Everything okay?"

Faith sighed and leaned back in the chair. "Of course things are okay. Why wouldn't they be okay?"

"Because you don't usually text me in the morning. What's going on?"

"Nothing." It was an honest answer, so she added, "That's the problem. I don't have a wedding this weekend, and everything else is done and I'm—"

"Bored."

Faith nodded. Her sister knew her well. "It's the craziest thing. I mean, I know it's only been a few weeks, but I think I'm actually getting used to this whole wedding thing."

"You mean, you're enjoying it?"

"No." She laughed, but it was sort of a lie. "But I don't totally hate it."

On the other end of the line, Hope gasped dramatically. "Did you just say that?"

"Don't tell anyone!"

"Your secret is safe with me, sis. Now fill me in on the gossip. I miss everyone."

Faith resisted the urge to tell her sister to come home if she missed them so much. That would be useless, so, instead, she did her best to fill her in on what as going on around town, as well as the details of Damon and Katie's super simple, but beautiful ceremony. She couldn't help but add that she herself had pulled off that wedding all on her own. It didn't matter that there were less than ten people in attendance.

"I still can't believe those two got married so quickly," Hope said. "I feel like it was just yesterday that Katie was telling us about it."

"So crazy." She shook her head. "But it seems to be working. Well, except last night was weird."

The night before *had* been weird, and normally Faith wouldn't have thought much about it, except they had all been gathered to raise their glasses in a toast to the happy newlyweds and then they'd both just taken off without an explanation, leaving everyone to wonder what exactly had happened.

"Weird how?"

"We were all celebrating with them, and then Katie went to the bathroom and Damon went to get more drinks." She didn't bother mentioning that he'd never come back with those drinks. "The last I saw him, he was talking to some guy at the bar."

"Some guy?"

Faith nodded. "We found out later he's a friend of Damon's from the city. He came over to introduce himself." She didn't bother telling her sister that Damon's friend, Nick, was super-hot and ridiculously flirty. "Anyway, I never did see Damon again, but Sarah said she saw Katie take off in a hurry, so…" She shrugged. "Like I said, it was weird."

"That does sound weird." The sisters talked it over for a few minutes, and then switched gears while Hope filled her in on their travels. They were currently in France, and it sounded absolutely heavenly. Faith had never given it much thought before, but maybe she should consider doing some travel on her own. She let her thoughts drift for a moment but the sound of a truck entering her yard distracted her.

"Hey, Hope?" Faith sat up straight in her chair as she looked out the window at her visitor. "I think I'm going to have to let you go."

"Why? What's—"

She didn't hear the rest of her sister's question because a second later, Logan Langdon, looking angrier than she'd ever seen him, flung open her kitchen door and crashed his way into her kitchen. "I'm going to fucking kill him!"

---

The rain was just starting to come down as Damon made his way down Main Street. Talking to his father had been a good start, but he still had more to do. But before he could do anything, he needed to think. And he couldn't do that at ElkView. So he'd made his way down to town and had started walking. He'd lingered outside Sweetie Pies but couldn't make himself go in. A honey bun would only remind him of Katie and the mess they were in. So he'd kept walking.

But it was no use, because every single thing in town reminded him of Katie. All of his memories were wrapped up in her. He walked past the Big Rock Inn where, only a few days ago, they'd had their first fight. She'd told him then that there was nothing going on with her and Jeremy. *Had she been lying?* In his heart, if he could see past his jealousy, Damon knew she hadn't been lying to him. Katie *never* lied to him.

He'd overreacted.

He'd ruined everything.

And he knew it.

What he didn't know was how to make it right. She hadn't answered any of his phone calls or texts all morning, and although he knew he could drive over to her ranch and demand that she talk to him, he also knew that approach would probably not go over well with her. Or her family.

"Hey, Banks!"

Damon's head shot up to see his buddy Nick walking out the front door of the Big Rock Inn. He instantly felt a flash of guilt. He'd forgotten about Nick, and that was a shitty thing to do considering Nick had come to Glacier Falls for him.

"Where the hell did you go last night?" Nick joined him on the sidewalk. "Don't tell me that dude was—"

"I don't want to talk about it."

"No way." Nick shook his head. "Shit, Damon. I was kidding. I didn't think that your new bride really would—"

"She didn't!" His temper flared, but he caught himself. "Sorry, Nick. I didn't mean to take it out on you. And I'm sorry for leaving without saying anything last night. I just…"

Nick slapped his shoulder. "Don't worry about it, man. Really. I found your friends and introduced myself."

Damon couldn't help but smile. Of course Nick would have made himself at home.

"You didn't tell me about the blonde hottie."

Damon looked at his friend in confusion. "The blonde…"

"Yay tall…" Nick held out his hand. "Curvy, sexy, blue eyes, and…hey, she looks a lot like that woman."

Damon turned to see Logan's truck, with Faith in the passenger seat, screech to a halt in front of them. He registered the look on Logan's face, only seconds before the man flung the truck door open and ran toward him.

"What the fuck, Banks?" He lunged for him, but somehow Damon managed to dodge him. Nick, who'd initially only had eyes for Faith, jumped into action, and put himself between the hulking angry man and his buddy. "Move," Logan growled. "Or I'll go through you."

"Whoa." Nick held his hands up. "I think we should all calm down."

Damon's mind raced, but he didn't have to think too hard to know exactly what Logan was mad about. *Katie.* He just didn't know *what* about Katie Logan was mad about. "You need to talk to me, Logan. What's going on?"

"Logan, stop it!" Faith joined Nick standing between

Logan and the source of his anger. "You need to calm down. I'm sorry, Damon." She turned her head to look at him. "I tried to stop him, but he wouldn't listen."

"I'm going to kill you!"

"You aren't going to kill anyone." Faith turned back to him and to Damon's surprise, Logan's face actually softened a little when he looked at her. But not enough, because he still looked as though he did, in fact, intend to kill him.

"I don't know what you think I—"

"You fucking lied, Damon. About all of it."

*Ahh. So the truth was totally out.* Damon nodded once but didn't have time to speak.

"You used her." Logan wasn't done. "You hurt my little sister and that means you need to hurt."

"Enough!" Faith grabbed Logan by both arms and pushed him back a step to give them some distance.

Instead of using that distance, Damon stepped around Nick and toward Logan. "You're right," he said. "I did hurt her. But it wasn't my intention," he added quickly. "The last thing I would ever want is to hurt her, Logan."

Logan wasn't buying it. He shook his head and clenched his fists.

"It's true." Damon wouldn't have blamed the man if he punched him. Hell, he almost wanted Logan to punch him. He deserved it. But more than that, what he really wanted was to make things okay again. Better than okay. He needed everyone to know how he really felt and more than that, he needed *Katie* to know how he really felt. "I love her, Logan." The moment the words were out of his mouth, he smiled. And then despite himself and the situation he was in, he laughed and said it again. Louder this time. "I love her. I love Katie Langdon."

But then, just like that, the laughter was gone, and the smile dropped off his face as reality crashed back in. Damon stared at Logan, Faith, and Nick, who all looked at him as if he'd lost his mind. He scrubbed a hand over his face and tugged at his hair before speaking again. "I screwed up," he said as honestly as he could. "I know that." Logan snorted and shook his head, but Damon kept talking. "I need to fix things," he said. "And I think I'm going to need your help."

## Chapter Eighteen

"I CANNOT BELIEVE you talked me into this." Katie turned from the mirror where she'd been staring at her reflection for the last five minutes, to Faith, who'd just walked into her bedroom. It had been two days since the blow-up fight she'd had with Damon. And despite all the texts and phone calls from him that she'd ignored the morning after, she hadn't heard from him. Except once. The day before. An envelope had arrived by courier. It held the paperwork making the Hub legally hers. And a note:

*It always would have been yours. No matter what.*

She'd almost called him then. But she couldn't bring herself to do it. She was still so hurt.

What was almost as bad as not talking to Damon was that nobody was talking *about* him. At least not to her.

It was bizarre.

Especially because they all knew that the wedding was a

fake. Well, maybe they didn't *all* know. But Logan had over-heard her telling her mother, and of course he'd run off to tell Faith, whom, from what she understood, had talked him out of going to find Damon and punching him out. But beyond that little bit of information, no one had so much as mentioned Damon, the fact that they'd lied to everyone, or the fact that she was now living back at home.

And that's what was bizarre. It wasn't like her family not to push an issue, especially a major one. If she cared more, she might have asked them about it, but if she was being honest, Katie was enjoying the reprieve from reality when it came to Damon.

Except this.

She looked back to the mirror and once again took in the image of herself in her wedding dress, her hair done and her makeup carefully applied. This was a little too close to reality for her liking.

"You look gorgeous." Katie caught Faith's grin in the mirror's reflection. "Thank you for doing this. It's probably not the easiest thing to…" She let the thought drift away, which was probably for the best because there was definitely nothing easy about playing dress-up in her wedding gown—for a photo shoot, of all things—when her actual marriage was a complete and total train wreck.

To put it mildly.

"Well, I hope it helps," was all Katie could say. "Let's get this over with."

Faith had called the night before and asked whether she'd help her out with the photos for a new marketing campaign she'd been thinking about, and considering Katie really had nothing else to do but sit around and feel sorry for herself, she'd agreed. It was a choice she was regretting, especially because putting on the gown had brought back way more feel-ings than she'd expected it to. The last time she'd worn it, she'd married Damon. And despite the fact that it was all supposed to have been a big lie, it hadn't *felt* like a lie when she'd held his hands, looked in his eyes, and vowed to marry him. And that's because it wasn't a lie. It was the most honest thing she'd ever done.

Tears threatened to spill, but Katie refused to let them fall. She blinked hard and forced a smile and turned to face Faith, who seemed oblivious of the emotional tornado taking place inside her.

"This is going to be the best ad campaign ever." Faith grabbed her hand and led her from the room. "Hope will be so surprised when she sees it because I know she hasn't even thought about marketing on social media yet, and I don't understand why not." She stopped to grab her folder from the kitchen table, and without letting go of her hand, kept half dragging, half leading Katie from the kitchen and out to her waiting SUV. The entire time, she yammered on and on about ads and images and slogans, and Katie was really only half listening as she got into Faith's passenger seat.

Katie couldn't help but be impressed as Faith kept up a stream of chatter all the way to Ever After Ranch, barely pausing for her to react to anything she was saying. Which was probably for the best, because Katie couldn't imagine she would have much of a reaction at all. She was about to pretend that she was a bride, only days after her own marriage—real or not—had imploded. What would she say?

"Hey," she did say a moment later. "Where are we going?" They'd just driven past the main gates for Ever After, and were still headed down the gravel road. She tried to twist around in her seat. "You passed the gates."

"Oh, I know." Faith grinned at her. "We're going in the back gate. It's closer to the river and I want to get some pictures down there. Logan is meeting us with the quad and he'll take us around to the other sites after."

"The other sites?"

"Just the ceremony site and the barn."

Katie groaned.

"I know, I know. But it will be fun. I promise."

Katie stared out the window. There was no way any of it was going to be fun. But a promise was a promise. And she always kept her promises.

*And isn't that what got her into this predicament in the first place?*

---

Damon paced the length of the barn, and then again. He felt like a caged animal, unable to do anything but wait for his captor to let him out.

In this case, his captor might also prove to be his savior. Because when it was time, he'd get the text message saying everything was ready to go.

It was a huge plan and there was no way he would have been able to pull any of it off without his friends' help. He really owed them.

*If it worked.*

It had to work, because Damon had no idea what he was going to do if it didn't. The last few days without Katie had been hell. There was no way he could imagine a lifetime in that purgatory. He needed her just to exist. And he hadn't even realized it.

He'd almost broken down the night before and gone to see her, but ultimately forced himself to stay put. They'd put all the work in. All that was left was to execute. Besides, there was nothing that he could say that was going to be able to properly express to Katie how he felt. He needed to *show* her. He needed the big, huge, massive grand gesture. And that's what he was going to do. Because there was no other choice left.

Damon pulled his phone out of this pocket for the dozenth time to make sure he hadn't missed the text message.

He hadn't.

With a sigh, he put his hands on the bar and dropped his head.

"Son?"

Damon's head shot up to see his father in the doorway of the barn, leaning heavily on his walker. "Dad? Is everything okay? What are you—"

"I needed to tell you something."

Damon crossed the floor and led his dad to a nearby table, where he settled him into a chair. He had no idea what his dad could possibly have to tell him now that they'd set everything straight.

Anthony held out his hand, and Damon took it in his. It was the second time in as many days, but it still felt strange to hold his father's hand. But he welcomed the connection. And despite their strained relationship, the contact settled Damon.

"I'm proud of you, son."

His father said the words so simply and without any fanfare, but they resonated in Damon's head. Not once, not even when he'd designed and sold the microchip, had his father ever expressed anything resembling pride to him. He closed his eyes and bent his head, absorbing what he'd said. Even as a fully grown adult, the words still meant the world to him.

After a moment, he looked up. "Thank you, Dad."

"I mean it," Anthony said, a slight waver in his voice. "I haven't always been a good father, but you are a damn fine son, and you've grown into a man that any damn fool would be proud of. Especially today."

Damon couldn't help but shake his head a little. "There's still a lot left to happen today, Dad. We don't know how it's going to go. I don't know if she'll—"

"She will."

"We don't know that."

"No," Anthony said bluntly. "But no one knows the future, do they?"

Damon chuckled a little. "We certainly don't."

"All we can do is our best, son. And you're doing your best here today. And for that, I'm more proud of you than I've ever been before." He squeezed Damon's hand in his. "I love you, Damon, and your mother would be so proud of you today, too."

He pressed something into Damon's hand but before he had a chance to respond, or even wipe the tear that had developed in the corner of his own eye, his father struggled to his feet at the same time that his phone chirped with an incoming text.

*Go time.*

## Chapter Nineteen

FOR THE NEXT THIRTY MINUTES, Katie forced herself to smile and tried to look *bridal*—whatever that meant—as Faith took pictures of her standing by pine trees next to the river. Most of the time, she was able to convince herself that it was all business and for marketing purposes only, but more than once, she glanced down at her dress and tears welled up in her eyes as the memory of her standing with Damon as they exchanged vows rushed back in vivid detail.

"Faith, are we almost done?" Katie called out over her shoulder. Faith had directed her to put her arm up on a tree and gaze out over the river, but she hadn't given her any direction for a few minutes.

"Um…hold on."

Katie turned around and sighed. Faith wasn't even holding her camera. Instead, she was staring at her phone.

She'd had enough. This was torture. Katie left her tree and picked her way through the tall grass toward her friend, whose head shot up.

"Good timing. Let's go finish up."

"Finish up?" She groaned when she remembered what

Faith had said about taking some pictures at the ceremony site. "Seriously? We really have to do that?" She crossed her arms like a pouty teenager. "I'm not sure how much you know, but Damon and I—"

"Oh!" Faith interrupted her. "Logan's here. It'll be faster to go there in the golf cart. Ready?"

Katie sighed as her brother pulled up with the little golf cart that he and Faith used to move around the property. With a resigned sigh, she got into the backseat and closed her eyes. Maybe if she stopped protesting, they could get this over with faster.

A few minutes later, the cart slowed to a stop and Katie opened her eyes. She instantly closed them again and shook her head. "No."

"Come on," Faith said quickly. Obviously anticipating the objection, she'd turned around and grabbed Katie's hand. "I needed it to look real, and we needed guests for that."

"No." Katie shook her head again and forced herself not to cry. "Faith, I don't know how much you know about what happened with—" She tried again, but once again, Faith cut her off.

"Come on. It's just a few people. They're going to pretend to be guests."

It had looked like a lot more than just a few people, but Katie really didn't want to open her eyes again.

"Katie, it's not a big deal." Logan spoke up. "Besides, if we don't get these shots, it won't look real for the ad campaign."

Slowly, Katie opened her eyes and stared at her brother, whom, she noticed for the first time, wore a suit. "And I suppose you're going to be my pretend groom?"

Instead of answering, he laughed, jumped out of the cart, and held out his hand to her. "Come on."

"This is ridiculous." She pressed her lips into a line and shook her head.

"We're almost done," Faith pleaded. "Please?"

"You owe—" She cut off her own words. Faith didn't owe her anything. After all, she'd already thrown her a fake wedding, all because of Katie's lies. If anyone owed anyone anything, it was her. And she knew it.

She took her brother's hand. "Let's get this over with."

Katie tried not to make eye contact with the *guests* Faith had brought in for the shoot, but she did vaguely register Sarah and Brody as Logan, whose job clearly was to walk her down the aisle—probably so she didn't bolt—and not to be her pretend groom, started doing just that. She swallowed hard against the lump in her throat and sent a silent prayer for the photoshoot to end quickly.

"It'll be fine," Logan whispered into her ear. "Trust me." He winked at her and just before she could ask him why he was being weird, music started to play.

*Wedding music.*

This was too much. Sure, she could understand that Faith wanted it to look as real as possible, but *music?* It was all bordering on completely ridiculous.

She would have run, but Logan held her arm tight and started to walk down the aisle toward the front of the gorgeous ceremony space that was set up with a stunning arch, covered in fresh wild flowers and tulle that was blowing, just slightly, in the breeze. The sky had cleared, and the rain they'd had left everything fresh and greener than before. It was perfect. The only thing missing was the groom.

As if her thoughts had conjured him, Damon appeared, his father next to him. He didn't look up as he helped Anthony to a front-row seat, next to…her *mother?* When Mr. Banks was settled, Damon moved into position under the arch, turned around and looked directly at her.

She was gorgeous. Even more so than the first time he'd married her—if it were even possible.

He dropped his head briefly and took a deep breath. Everything was on the line with this. It needed to work. As he lifted his head again, he caught his buddy Nick's eye. Nick winked at him and nodded. It was such a small thing, but the support was appreciated and he was grateful that Nick had stuck around. He'd been a big help in pulling it all off.

He exhaled slowly and looked back to the love of his life, ready to do what it took.

Katie held tight to her brother's arm, and even though they were still a few feet away, Damon could see the way she shook and the look of question on her face. He held her gaze, doing his best to impart everything he was feeling for her in his eyes.

When they got close enough, he stepped forward. "Damon? What...the photo..." She looked to Logan, clearly trying to figure out what exactly was happening.

Logan shook his head and leaned forward to kiss her on the cheek. "It was our turn to lie," he said with a grin, before gently extracting himself from the situation, leaving the two of them alone—with everyone watching.

"Damon?" Tears pooled in her eyes.

Damon took hold of her hand. It shook in his, but he wasn't going to let it go. He dropped to one knee and smiled up at her.

"What are you doing?" She hissed at him under her breath. "This doesn't make sense."

"It does," he said. "This is the thing that makes the most sense. Katie, I love you."

"Damon, I know. I love you, too, but—"

"No, Katie." He had to make her see. "I'm *in* love with you. Madly, deeply, and completely crazy in love with you." He chuckled a little. "I can't even see straight most of the time when you're around. And I'm certainly not thinking right. I think that's clear from the way I've been behaving." He shook his head a little. "I don't even know how to properly explain this to you, Katie. But I'm going to try, okay?"

She didn't look convinced, but she nodded, just a little, and that was all Damon needed to keep going.

"You've always been my best friend. The one person in this world I couldn't imagine living without. I think I've always been in love with you, Katie, but I was too young and stupid to see it for far too long. We are more than good together." He noticed the way she winced at his choice of words, but it didn't deter him. "We are *everything* together.

"Marrying you last week was the best decision of my entire life." A tear slipped down her cheek and he resisted the urge to stand and wipe it away. He needed to finish first. "My only regret was that I didn't give you the wedding you deserved the first time." He swallowed hard. "No," he corrected himself. "That's not my only regret. My biggest regret was trying to pretend it wasn't real, because it was. You and I are the most real thing I've ever had in my life and I need you to know that, Katie. I love you with all of my heart and more than anything, I want to spend the rest of my life proving that to you." He took a deep breath. "Will you marry me?"

There were a few gasps of surprise and muttering from the crowd that he'd almost forgotten was still there. Surely, the truth had spread through them all by that point—not that Damon cared what Faith and Logan had told them to get them there, as long as they were there. Katie had told him all about the wedding she'd imagined she would have and that's exactly what he was going to give her.

If she said yes.

"Damon, I…"

"Tell me that you don't love me." From his pocket, Damon pulled the ring his father had given him earlier. His mother's wedding band. He squeezed it briefly, took a breath, and held it up. "Tell me that you don't feel the same way, Katie. And if you do, I promise I'll get up and walk away. But I need to hear you say it."

She was silent for a moment before dropping her head but still, Damon waited. After what felt like forever, she looked up and grinned. "I can't," she said. "I can't say that because it's not true. Damon, I *do* love you. You make me crazy and make me want to tear my hair out sometimes, but I can't imagine my life without you in it."

Her lips flicked up into a smile and his heart about burst in his chest.

"So, that's a—"

"Yes!" She shook her hand in his. "A thousand times yes. I will...*stay* married?" She laughed, but there would be time to work out the semantics of everything.

For now, Damon had heard all he needed to.

He slipped the ring onto Katie's finger—where it had always belonged—jumped to his feet, and pulled her into his arms before pressing his lips to hers in the kiss he'd been dying to give her since he'd seen her.

When they finally pulled apart, he kissed her again. And then again.

## Chapter Twenty

FAITH TOOK in a deep breath of the fresh spring air. The noise from inside filtered out to her and made her smile, but she was happy to have a break from the festivities, even if it was just for a few minutes, to compose herself and regroup.

It was days like this one that made Faith miss her sister so much her chest ached.

*Had she handled things okay? Should she have lied to Katie the way she had? Should she have...* The *shoulds* threatened to actually drive her crazy. Which was ridiculous, because it had all worked out okay. More than okay. Damon and Katie were desperately in love—something everyone else had seen for years—and finally they both saw it *and* they were married.

Sure, there'd been a few hiccups—massive understatement —but it had all turned out beautifully in the end. The reception had been in full swing for just over an hour. People were fed, they were drinking and laughing, and the dance would start soon.

There'd been no further issues.

Still. Faith knew Hope would have handled things so much better. She probably would have noticed right away that things weren't what they seemed. It never would have gotten so far. She was always on top of everything, so organized, and so aware of people. Faith didn't have those skills. She'd always been the self-centered one. The one who only thought about herself. Her twin sister had gotten all of the selfless traits. Among others.

Faith sat in one of the wrought-iron chairs that were primarily used for decoration and pulled her phone out. No doubt Hope and Levi were in the middle of a grand adventure over in Europe, living their best life while they waited for the happy news that they were finally pregnant, the perfect complement to the love the two of them shared.

Faith couldn't help but feel a twinge of jealousy but she couldn't determine where it had come from. Was it the fact that Hope was out traveling the world while she was stuck in Glacier Falls, planning weddings? Was it that she was trying for a baby? Or was it the love she had with Levi?

It was ridiculous for her to feel jealousy for any of those things. She'd never wanted any of them. Except maybe travel…but love, marriage, and a baby?

Oh hell, no.

*Still.*

She pressed the button that would dial her sister. If she was in the middle of something, too bad. Faith needed her.

Hope answered on the first ring.

"Hey. What's up?" Her voice instantly soothed Faith the way only a twin sister could. "Is everything okay?"

Faith laughed. "It is. And you'll never believe it when I tell you about it."

She spent the next few minutes filling Hope in on the details and when she was done, Hope exhaled hard. "Damn, Faith. You nailed it. Good job."

"I don't think I can take all of the credit. Logan was super helpful."

"He was? That's good to hear."

There was a tone in her sister's voice that Faith made a distinct point to ignore. She had enough mixed feelings about the man, feelings that had only grown even more confusing as she'd watched him work so hard for his sister's wedding. A wedding he'd been so dead set against at the beginning. *Maybe love really did get to everyone in the end?*

"I'll admit," she continued, "I had my reservations about the two of you working together, but to hear he's been helpful…that makes me feel better."

Sure, he'd been *helpful*. Helpful in stirring up feelings in her that should have stayed buried forever. Helpful in distracting her from her mission to never let herself care about anyone else.

She shook her head from the thought. "I wish you'd been here, Hope," she said honestly. "You would have known what to—"

"Don't do that." Her sister cut her off. "You're more than capable of handling this. And by the sounds of it, you more than proved it. You need to give yourself more credit. Really."

Faith nodded. "Maybe you're right. I'll try to enjoy myself a little."

"Good."

"I miss you right now," Faith said honestly a moment later. "What are you guys doing? You're probably getting ready to have some amazing lunch at a cafe in Paris or something, right?"

Hope laughed a little. "Well, that would be hard since we're actually—"

"Don't tell me." Faith interrupted her. "You're on the Eiffel Tower right now, aren't you? Take so many—"

"We're actually just at the hospital." Hope interrupted her. "But I don't want you to worry, Faith. It's—"

"Hospital?" Faith sat up in her chair. "What the hell, Hope? Are you okay?"

"I am," she said quickly. "Honestly, I am. I was just feeling really tired and a little weak so we wanted to get my levels checked out and make sure everything was okay, so they ran a few tests, that's all."

She knew it had been a bad idea for Hope to go traveling instead of having the surgery that would get rid of her uterine cancer. Her sister was rolling the dice with her life, trying to have a baby before seeking the treatment she needed, and it made Faith crazy. And now…she was in the hospital thousands of miles away. It was definitely *not* okay.

"You need to come home, Hope. Don't know if being over there is—"

"I'm fine." She interrupted Faith again. "Honestly. Levi is taking good care of me." She laughed. "In fact, he's probably more of a pain in the ass than you are about making sure I'm eating and sleeping. I'm in good hands."

That was probably true and even though Faith would have liked to be the one making sure her sister was taking care of herself, she knew that Levi loved her just as much. He wouldn't let anything happen to her.

Still, she was going to protest again when she heard the sounds of the DJ inside the barn getting ready to announce the first dance. "Okay," Faith finally relented. "I'll trust Levi to take care of you. But let me know when you get the test results back, okay?"

"I promise. I love you, Faith. Now get back to that wedding. And give them both a hug from us."

---

Katie and Damon had just taken to the dance floor by the time Faith made her way inside. She leaned up against a wooden pillar to watch the dance that, from the very second the music started, was arguably one of the most romantic she'd ever seen. There was no mistaking the love they had for each other.

"It almost makes you wish it were you, right?" Logan slipped an arm around her and pulled her close.

*Were they really that comfortable with each other now?*

Instinctively, she pulled away and crossed her arms.

"Whoa." Logan chuckled. "You're either still mad at me for being against all this at the beginning, or—and I think this is more likely—you're still not ready to admit you're in to me."

She glared at him. "I am *not* in to you."

It was a lie and they both knew it.

"If you say so." Logan shrugged and focused on the couple on the dance floor.

She watched his face for a moment as he watched his little sister with her new husband. It was nice to see him more relaxed with the idea of Damon and Katie together, particularly after the way things had gone down. Judging by the smile on his face, he'd obviously come to terms with it, too.

"It was really nice of you to help out, Logan," Faith blurted. "I know you weren't happy with the whole thing."

He half turned so he could still keep an eye on the dance floor while he answered her. "I wasn't," he started. "But I could see it, too."

"See what?"

"Their love," he answered simply. "And I may not have the most experience with this kind of stuff, but I'm not completely dead inside." The comment stung, but he didn't seem to notice. "They're perfect for each other, and...well, what's the point of fighting that? Especially when they're so happy?"

She nodded and looked at him in wonder. Never in a million years would she have thought that Logan Langdon was a closet romantic. *If Logan could see past his own hardness to appre-*

*ciate love, then maybe there was still hope for her. Could there be hope for her and Log—*

"Not everyone is a love 'em and leave 'em type like you, Faith."

She recoiled at his comment, warm thoughts vanished. "Pardon?"

He turned and crossed his arms over his chest. "I'm just saying, it does kind of seem to be your MO, doesn't it?" Before she could answer, he added, "At least the other guy got close enough to you to be left. I can't even get that far."

"What?" She bristled. "The *other guy*?"

His smile was completely gone now. "Yeah, the guy you left in the city when you came back here. Nothing serious there either, right?"

*Noah. He was talking about Noah.* Leaving him hadn't been easy, but Noah had known the deal, too. Nothing serious. She didn't *do* relationships. She'd never led anyone on. She'd always been straightforward. She wasn't going to change.

"I don't need to explain anything to you, Logan." She turned away and looked back to the dance floor, but Logan wasn't done.

"No," he said. "You don't. And I know, you were pretty clear with how you felt about everything." She turned to look at him again. "But I think you're full of shit. In fact, I think this whole little *I don't love anyone* act that you have going on is just that—one big act." His lips curled up into a cocky grin that was equal parts deadly and infuriating. "And I intend to prove it."

He turned and left, making his way onto the dance floor right as the family dances started, so smoothly, Faith was left dumbfounded in his wake. *What the hell was he talking about? Prove what? Damn, he made her blood boil.* He always had. It had been a mistake letting those feelings of annoyance turn into anything else.

Especially desire.

She closed her eyes and gave herself a moment to compose herself. She needed to clear her mind. She still had a wedding to coordinate. She didn't have time to think about Logan or what feelings she may or may not have. She scanned the room and her gaze landed on Brody standing by the kitchen door, looking out into the room. But he wasn't watching the festivities; his gaze was locked on one person in particular.

Sarah.

Faith couldn't help but smile.

Clearly, she *was* starting to be affected by all this wedding and forever after hoopla.

She moved silently and quickly to the other side of the room. "Dinner was fantastic, Brody. Everyone was impressed. And doing it so quickly like that? I owe you."

"It was my pleasure, and you definitely don't owe me." He nodded but didn't look at her for a moment. Finally, he turned. "It's a beautiful wedding. They all are. It makes you think, doesn't it?"

"Does it?" Faith took a step back before looking across the room to where Sarah was watching the dances continue. "Is there something you're not telling me, Brody?"

"No, no." Brody laughed. "Not at all. But look at this." Brody dug into his pocket and held out the most beautiful ruby ring she'd ever seen.

"Brody!"

"Do you think she'll like it?"

"Sarah? Of course. But, are you going to—"

"Oh my God, no!" Brody exclaimed when he realized what Faith was thinking. "It's just a gift. My mom sent it with a box full of things that used to belong to my grandmother and... well, I just thought..."

Faith raised her eyebrows. "You thought what?"

"I thought Sarah would like it. She was the first person I thought of when I saw it. Ruby is Rory's birthstone and—"

"She'll love it." Faith grinned at him. "And I think you two will make a super cute couple."

"Couple?" He shook his head. "We're just friends, Faith."

*Friends. Right.*

She smiled and didn't bother pushing it as she watched him disappear back into the kitchen. One day the two of them would realize they were more than just friends. Really, if *she* of all people could see it, surely they'd figure it out soon?

Faith laughed. She didn't even recognize herself thinking about love so much. This wedding business was *definitely* getting to her.

Feeling a little outside of herself, she once more turned to survey the room.

It felt as though everyone was falling prey to this whole *love* charade.

Was everyone around her going crazy?

Or was it her? Was *she* missing something?

She needed a drink.

Faith was just about to go in search of a glass of champagne, or more likely, something stronger, when her phone chirped with an incoming text message.

It was Hope.

*The test results.*

Anxiously, she pulled her phone free from her pocket.

*Test results are in....I'm pregnant!*

---

**I hope you enjoyed Ever After Ranch and Katie and Damon's love story. But wait! What happened after the festivities? Click here for an exclusive bonus**

scene and find out what happened on the wedding
night!

And next, can a single mom who's guarding an old
hurt, open her heart long enough to let love in? Brody
and Sarah's journey to love is next, in Wanting
Happily Ever After.
Read a sneak peek right after this.

## Wanting Happily Ever After

Please enjoy this excerpt from the third in the Ever After Series—*Wanting Happily Ever After*

It was hot. The kind of hot that made sitting on metal bleachers, shoulder to shoulder with dozens of other parents, a special kind of torture, especially when what you should be doing was sitting in the shade by the river with your feet in the water and a cold drink in your hand. But that wasn't an option for Sarah Lewis, not with her six-year-old daughter, Rory, running down the length of the soccer field, her teammates and friends next to her, long braids streaming behind her as she moved as fast as she could toward the goal.

For the life of her, Sarah could not imagine how any of them had so much energy on such a hot July afternoon, but none of the kids looked nearly as wilted as the parents. And if they could do it…she stood and cheered as loud as she could as Rory kicked the ball toward the net. There was no way the ball would go in. It was headed straight to the center of the goal… and the opposing team's goalie, who looked to be at least twice the size of the rest of the team. She'd easily be able to stop it.

Sarah clutched her hands together and mentally prepared herself for Rory's disappointment.

The ball moved, almost in slow motion. The goalie made her move. She opened her arms and jumped...right over the ball. Before anyone even realized what had happened, the ball was in the net and the referee blew the whistle, making it official.

Sarah exchanged glances with two of the other parents, Myrna and Jocelyn, on either side of her. The other mothers shook their heads in disbelief for a moment before leaping up and cheering. The team had just won! The Glacier Falls Grizzlies were going to play in the championship game!

Both the kids on the field and the parents and spectators in the stands erupted in cheers and screaming. Sarah watched as the realization of what had just happened hit her daughter. Rory's six-year-old face transformed. She dropped her hands momentarily to her knees. Her head dangled for a moment before she looked up, lifted her arms in the air, and let out a whoop of joy.

"She did it. She really did it." She shook her head and laughed at herself. After all, it was just a summer league child's soccer game, but she couldn't contain her excitement. It was a big deal to Rory, which meant it was a big deal to her.

"She did awesome!" Jocelyn wrapped her in a quick hug. "The girls played so well this season."

Sarah nodded and her gaze traveled across the field to where the team had met in a quick huddle to cheer their opposition and go shake hands. Her eyes landed on the coach, towering above his little players, a ball cap on his head to shield him from the sun, a matching red jersey, with "Coach" emblazoned on the back, right under "Birchwood," the name of the team's corporate sponsor—and the head coach's restaurant. Brody Morris held his ever-present clipboard in hand, and used it as a prop to wave in the air as the girls ran through their three cheers and went to shake hands with the other team. A fluttering sensation landed in her stomach when he turned toward her and raised his free hand in a small wave. A sensation that was happening more and more frequently lately. After all, he *was* very good-looking. Especially when he was playing the role of super coach.

"He's the best coach we've ever had," Myrna said, distracting her from staring at Brody.

"He really stepped up," someone else said.

"We're pretty lucky that you're dating Brody Morris, Sarah."

Her stomach fell, the flutterings squashed as Sarah whipped around to see who'd spoken. Audrey Hill smiled sweetly at Sarah, but there was nothing sweet intended by the comment, and they both knew it.

"We're not dating." Sarah hated that she even had to say something, particularly to Audrey. But if she didn't say anything, the rumors would start. And knowing Audrey, in less than twenty-four hours, the entire town would have heard that Sarah and Brody were not only a hot couple, but that they were expecting twins and moving in together, or something equally ludicrous. It didn't even matter if it wasn't based in truth; Audrey had a special gift of starting trouble. Trouble that, for whatever reason, she liked to aim in Sarah's direction.

It didn't help that Audrey's little girl, Clara, was Rory's favorite playmate.

"Well, you sure spend a lot of time together," Audrey continued, her voice carefully measured. "So if that's not dating, I don't know what is."

Sarah came up with a hundred different comebacks, but ultimately, shook her head and decided not to say anything. Audrey Hill wasn't worth it. Instead, she turned away, and looked straight at Byron Smith, single dad of Annie, one of

Rory's teammates. He smiled kindly, as if to offer support, but Sarah couldn't help but think there was more behind his smile.

Byron had asked her out on more than one occasion and every time, Sarah had come up with an excuse. It wasn't that Byron wasn't a nice man. He really was. But…it was always something. At first, it was because she just wasn't ready to date. And then, after a while…there was Brody. She hadn't lied to Audrey; they really weren't dating. They were friends. Best friends. And even if she did get that ridiculous fluttering feeling in her gut when he was around, it didn't matter because Brody would never be more than a friend. She valued him in her life too much for that. No way was she going to screw things up by dating. Even if she was open to that—which she wasn't.

She snuck a glance over to where Brody was gathering up the equipment on the sidelines and her stomach fluttered again.

*No.*

She wasn't going there. And definitely not with Brody.

Sarah knew she was her own worst enemy when it came to overthinking the situation, but she couldn't help it.

Thankfully, Rory saved her from any further thinking on the subject and chose that moment to holler up at her. "Mom! Did you see that, Mom?"

"I sure did, kiddo!" Without another look at anyone, Sarah gathered up her bag and made her way down the bleachers toward her daughter. She picked her up and squeezed her. "You were awesome. The game-winning goal! Wow."

"Wow indeed." Sarah's father, Ed Walker, appeared and Rory clambered into his arms. "Good job, Rory. I'm so proud of you."

"I didn't know you were here, Dad."

With a kiss on her head, Ed put his granddaughter down and she ran off to sit with her team in the shade of a tree to eat orange slices and celebrate their win. "I got here right after the second half started," he said. "Sorry I was late. I lost track of time in the garage."

Her dad had always been a putterer, with more projects than Sarah could keep straight. He still worked as Glacier Falls' fire chief, but more and more, Sarah could see that what he really wanted to focus on were his countless projects. And his granddaughter. Ed was a grade-A grandfather. He never missed an important date, but more importantly, he never missed anything Rory thought was important.

"Do you think she noticed I was late?" Ed looked with concern to the little girl, who didn't look as if she had a care in the world.

"You were here for the most important part and that's all that matters." She gave her dad a quick hug. "Thanks for coming. It means the world, Dad."

"You know I wouldn't miss it."

She did know. Still, it was worth saying, and she didn't like to miss an opportunity to tell her father how much she appreciated him.

After Sarah's mom died when she was barely a toddler, it had just been the two of them. And then, after the accident that had left Sarah a widow five years earlier, when Rory was only a baby, Sarah had leaned heavily on her father.

"Wasn't that a great game?" Brody, clipboard still in hand, appeared next to her. Sarah couldn't help but notice how he always made a point to greet her before any of the other parents. It was a detail that didn't seem to be lost on anyone, her father included. Next to her, Ed tensed ever so slightly. "What did you think of that, Mr. Walker? Pretty great game, wasn't it?"

"It was pretty close there until the end." Ed crossed his arms over his chest, but his lips twitched up into a flicker of smile before it disappeared again. "It's a good thing that granddaughter of mine is so quick."

She didn't know what it was, but it didn't seem to matter what Brody did or said; her father didn't seem to like him very much. She couldn't figure it out because Brody had been a great friend to her over the last few months. He'd been nothing but helpful and kind and…she forced herself to stop the line of thinking she was on as the fluttering in her stomach made a reappearance.

"That is a good thing, Mr. Walker," Brody answered diplomatically. "She's a very talented little girl." He turned to smile at Sarah. It was a simple action, but it warmed her. "I should go make my rounds," he said to her. "But I'll give you a call later. I have an ice cream cake in the freezer at the restaurant that needs to be tested, and I thought Rory might want to help out."

Sarah laughed. "Oh, I think she'd love to help you out with that."

"Sounds good." Brody put his hand on her arm and squeezed.

*Did he hold it just a moment longer than was necessary?* If Sarah had any experience with men at all, she might know. But beyond her late husband, she'd never even dated. She smiled as he took his leave and went to talk to the other parents, who were all waiting to congratulate their star coach.

She watched as he was swallowed up by them with cheers and pats on the back before turning back to her father. Ed's mouth was still turned down in a frown. She stopped herself before reminding her dad, just like everyone else, that she wasn't dating Brody. Because even though he hadn't said as much, Sarah was pretty sure that was her father's issue. Just as he'd remained single, it seemed that he thought his daughter should do the same. But he didn't have to worry—she had no intention of coupling up again. Like father, like daughter.

Suddenly exhausted and overwhelmed by the heat, she shook her head and ignored her dad and whatever it was that he clearly wanted to say. "I'm melting," she said instead. "Let's go celebrate Rory's goal with some iced tea."

---

Brody Morris tried to stay focused on the parents who were showering him with completely undeserved praise. After all, it was youth summer league soccer, not the World Cup. First place prize was a medal. The same as every other place. But to the parents of Glacier Falls, his adopted hometown, he might as well have been training their daughters for the Olympics.

"What do you think their odds of winning are, Coach?"

"That team from Cedar Springs is pretty tough."

"I heard they have a ringer."

"A ringer? Does anyone check the birth certificates of these kids?"

Brody handled each of the questions, with a smile and a chuckle. "Win or lose, you should all be so proud of your girls out there. They're playing their hearts out and having so much fun," he said good-naturedly. "They're all great kids. We should celebrate that."

"And their championship," Audrey Hill said confidently. "I mean, it's obvious that they're going to win. We should plan a party as a wrap-up."

Brody shook his head, but did his best not to look disagreeable. He'd met women like Audrey Hill before, and he knew well enough to stay on their good side. The last thing he wanted or needed was to be involved in any kind of drama, or to have Audrey Hill on his bad side, which would be worse. He tried to sneak a glance at Sarah, but she was turned away from him, kneeling on the grass, helping Rory unlace her cleats. Sarah had mentioned once or twice that Audrey had mastered the art of passive-aggressive bitchiness. Something about *mean girl* syndrome or something like that. Whatever it was, Brody believed her and did his best to keep Audrey at arm's length.

"A wind-up party sounds like a great idea." He smiled. "Let me know the details."

"Oh, I thought maybe Sarah could organize it." Her voice dripped with a false sweetness. "After all, she didn't bring team snacks as much as everyone else. It's really the least she could do."

Brody noticed a few of the other parents roll their eyes and shake their heads in disbelief, but not one of them said anything. He knew, just as well as they all knew, that Sarah did her best to attend all of the games and practices. But there were a few times when she wasn't able to make it due to work because she was a single mom who essentially supported and raised her little girl by herself. Obviously that little detail wasn't about to be recognized by this group.

He usually bit his tongue, in an effort to remain a neutral party as much as possible, but this was too much. "You know Sarah does her best to be here whenever she can. She has a lot on her plate."

Audrey took a step back and raised her eyebrow. "Sounds like someone is getting a little defensive." She clucked her tongue. "I didn't mean to stir up anything."

That's *exactly* what she'd meant. Still, Brody kept a smile on his face. "Oh, of course, Audrey. All I'm saying is that Sarah—"

"Makes sure that her father brings the team snacks when she can't be here. And has never missed once."

Brody turned to see Sarah, speaking about herself in the third person, walk up to the group. He tried, but failed, to stifle a smile.

"And I'm pretty sure you know, Audrey, that my father brings Rory's snacks on *all* the days that I get caught up at work. After all, the snacks are assigned by *child* and not by *parent.* Isn't that right?"

Audrey stammered and struggled over her words, but finally swallowed hard and nodded curtly. "I was just—"

"Oh, I know what you were doing," Sarah continued, a sweet smile on her face. Only her crossed arms over her chest gave away her true feelings about the woman.

Brody couldn't help but be impressed by her self-restraint.

"And yes, if you're unable to host the wind-up party, by all means, I'd be more than happy to take it off your plate."

"Oh, that's not...I wasn't saying that—"

"No, no," Sarah continued. "I don't mind at all. I know how busy you are with..." She tilted her head and innocently asked, "What is it that keeps you so busy?"

Brody couldn't help it; a chuckle slipped out of his mouth. He tried to cover it with a cough, but he couldn't be sure it worked. Not that anyone paid him any attention. All eyes were on Audrey.

"Well." The other woman pulled herself up and pushed her shoulders back. "I don't think—"

"Don't worry about a thing." Sarah waved her hand casually. "I'll take care of all the details." She beamed at the other parents, who were all watching the little drama unfold. "I'll sort out some details on my end and send out an email. Have a great day, everyone." And just like that, she spun on her heel and, with her head held high, walked away.

Like all of the others, Brody watched her go with sheer amazement on his face. He couldn't help but notice the way Byron Smith was watching Sarah particularly closely. Brody forced himself not to let it bother him. Of course there'd be men interested in her. After all, she was an amazing woman. Strong, hardworking, and gorgeous—even though she clearly had no idea how good-looking she was. He'd been spending more and more time with Sarah since moving to Glacier Falls, and he was really enjoying getting to know her.

He'd been attracted to her instantly, but it didn't take long to learn that she was a dedicated single mom whose entire life was devoted to her little girl. It hadn't put Brody off, though; it had only made him more cautious. Maybe too cautious, because he'd clearly been friend-zoned. Hell, from what he could tell, every man had been friend-zoned. Sarah didn't seem the least bit interested in dating. But at least he had her as his closest friend. And that was something. But as much as Brody did know about Sarah, she still had a few surprises up her sleeve. And dealing with mean moms was an impressive skill, to say the least.

He made small talk for a few more minutes, gave high fives to all the kids and took his own leave shortly after.

It was hot, and he would have loved to spend the rest of the day sitting in the shade somewhere, preferably with his feet in the water, underneath the cool branches of a pine tree in the forest, but it was not to be. He had a restaurant to run, and despite his wildest dreams, Birchwood wasn't yet running itself.

The moment he stepped inside the restaurant, he knew something was wrong. If it was hot outside, it was an absolute sauna inside the walls. He went immediately to the thermostat on the wall, and groaned. He tapped at it, the extent of his knowledge of how to make it work again.

"Shit."

The last thing he needed was one more thing that wasn't working. Not when his list was already growing beyond the scope of things he would be able to handle—or afford. But air conditioning was going to have to go on the list. When he moved to Glacier Falls from his small town in rural Saskatchewan, he never would have expected it to get so hot in the middle of the summer. After all, wasn't it supposed to be cool in the middle of the mountains? Apparently not so much.

Not that he minded. At least, he wouldn't have minded the heat if the air conditioning wasn't broken.

How was he supposed to serve customers when it was so hot?

He pushed his way into the kitchen, where it must have been at least ten degrees warmer, if it were even possible.

"Tell me you brought a repair guy?" Amy, his head chef, greeted him from behind the stove. "I feel like I'm going to pass out."

"How long has it been broken?" Forgoing his usual chef jacket, Brody grabbed an apron and tied it around his waist. "This is crazy."

"You're telling me." Amy wiped her brow and leaned against the counter. "I was going to get some stock started, but I think I might just abandon that plan altogether."

"Agreed. Try not to use the stove or the oven for anything. Maybe we can offer a special cool summer menu?" His brain started to spin with ideas as he spoke. "We can do a gazpacho, and salads, of course. Maybe a ceviche and some sushi rolls."

"I like it." Amy switched off the stove and her attempt at stock. "Especially if it keeps me even a little bit cool."

"And for dessert, I'll whip up some sorbets and maybe another ice cream cake."

"*Another* ice cream cake?" Amy wiggled her eyebrows.

Brody had hired her about three months ago, and they'd become quick friends. She was a few years younger than he was, fresh out of a basic culinary program in the city and she'd proved to be not only a lot of fun to spend his days with, but also an incredibly talented chef. It was only a matter of time before he lost her to bigger and better things. He would miss her on a professional level and as a close friend when that day came.

"Don't think I didn't notice that cake in the freezer," she

continued. "I also noticed the note on it that said not to touch."

"It was a test cake."

"Riiigght." Amy rolled her eyes. "A *test* cake. Interesting that it also happens to be mint chocolate chip."

"Why is that interesting?"

"Oh, only because I happen to know that mint chocolate chip is a certain little girl's favorite flavor."

Brody turned to look at his friend. "And how do you know that's Rory's favorite flavor?"

"It's every little girl's favorite flavor, isn't it?"

She shot him a look, but Brody wasn't imagining the blush he saw on his friend's face. Sarah had mentioned more than once that Amy had been spending quite a bit of time around Rory's auntie, Nicole. Brody definitely wasn't going to ask, because it wasn't his business, but judging by Amy's reaction, his suspicions were correct and there was something more than friendship going on between the two.

"Sure it is." He winked. "But you're right. It is Rory's favorite, and I was going to take it over there later. But first, let me pull together some type of hot weather menu." He moved to leave Amy in the kitchen, to head into his tiny office, when she stopped him.

"Don't forget to call a repair man."

He flinched, hoping she couldn't see his reaction. "Of course. I'll find time to call a repair man." He dropped his head and rubbed his temple as he mentally added, *And the money to pay for it.*

**Will these two be able to bridge the gap between friends and lovers? Find out. Wanting Happily Ever After, Sarah and Brody's story is next!**

## About the Author

Elena Aitken is a USA Today Bestselling Author of more than forty romance and women's fiction novels. The mother of 'grown up' twins, Elena now lives with her very own mountain man in the heart of the very mountains she writes about. She can often be found with her toes in the lake and a glass of wine in her hand, dreaming up her next book and working on her own happily ever after.

*To learn more about Elena:*
www.elenaaitken.com
elena@elenaaitken.com